Dream Spinner

Dream Spinner

Joanne Hoppe

MORROW JUNIOR BOOKS
New York

1 2 3 4 5 6 7 8 9 10

Library of Congress Cataloging-in-Publication Data
Hoppe, Joanne. Dream spinner / Joanne Hoppe.   p.   cm.
Summary: When her family moves to an old house after her father remarries, fifteen-year-old Mary becomes increasingly immersed in dreams involving the people who lived in the house over one hundred years before.
ISBN 0–688–08559–8 (trade)
[1. Dreams—Fiction.   2. Space and time—Fiction.
3. Stepfamilies—Fiction.]   I. Title
PZ7.H7786Dr   1992   [Fic]—dc20   92–5258   CIP   AC

FOR THE DEAR CHILDREN:

- *Mark Stephen*
- *Amanda Elizabeth*
- *Melissa Jane*
- *Margaret Joanne*

While we sleep here, we are awake elsewhere,
and in this every man is two men.

∾JORGE LUIS BORGES

Dream Spinner

Chapter 1

A long, tree-lined driveway formed a leafy tunnel leading back to the house. It was gloomy in the fading light of an early August evening.

"This is it!" In the front seat, Annie quickly opened the door and jumped out. "I can't wait for you to see it!"

This is it? Mary Barrone could not believe it. She didn't move as her father opened his door and started after Annie, who would soon be his wife. She just sat and stared at what could be her new home.

The house loomed against the sky. It was a faded yellow with peeling green trim. Over the long thin windows were moldings that were shaped like eyebrows. The glass was black; the windows were sightless eyes. The center front was three stories high. At the top a peaked roof extended out on both sides. It looked like an odd hat that had been set down on the third story. The rest of the house was two stories, and elaborate gingerbread trim covered the roofline.

"You coming?" Brian, Annie's ten-year-old son, had gotten out of the car, but was leaning back in, looking at Mary.

"I suppose I have to," Mary said, slowly pushing down the door handle.

"Gee!" Brian's eyes were big behind his round, wire-framed glasses. "It's spooky-looking."

"No it isn't." Mary did not want to align herself with Brian. "It's just old. Just an ugly old house."

"Hurry up, kids!" Annie was standing on the front steps gesturing to them. "We don't have a lot of daylight left, and I want to show you *everything!* You'll love it. You'll just love, love, love it!"

"I'll bet," Mary muttered loud enough for Brian to hear. The grass was overgrown and scratched her legs as they walked across the lawn.

"Mary thinks it's ugly," Brian told the adults.

So he was going to be a tattletale. Mary had expected as much.

"I'm sure Mary will give it a chance," her father said. "Wait until you see the inside. We've never had so much room."

"I think it's creepy," Brian said. "Do we have to live here?"

"We want you and Mary to like it," Annie said. "That's why we brought you to see it before we signed the contract." She took an oversized key from her purse and fitted it into one side of the double front doors. The knob rattled loosely as she turned it, and the left door swung in. Cold, stale air greeted them.

"It could use an airing," John Barrone said.

"Phew, it stinks!" Brian put his hand to his nose.

"An elderly lady lived here for twenty years after her husband died," Annie said. "She had cats." She laughed. "I guess she had a lot of cats. We'll get rid of the smell, don't worry."

They were in a large front hall. The floor was dusty, and strips of wallpaper, curled at the edges, hung from places in the wall. Mary's father didn't seem to notice.

"Look at this banister," he said. "It must be original. Wonderful carving."

"Isn't it great?" Annie agreed. "And look at those French doors with that beautiful frosted glass. They lead to the parlor. Victorians had parlors, not living rooms, nothing so vulgar. They were quite stuffy, of course, but we won't be stuffy."

"You couldn't be stuffy if you tried." John Barrone smiled at Annie with an expression Mary resented. He seemed to think Annie was so cute.

"This is a real deal, John," Annie said. "I've been in real estate in Sound Port for ten years, and I've never seen a bargain like this—cats or no cats. Come on! Let's go upstairs. I'm dying to show Mary her room."

Annie bounded up the stairs ahead of them. Mary looked at her plump rear, which jiggled in the polka-dotted stirrup pants she was wearing. Gross, she thought.

∽ 3

"Have we got a surprise for you!" Annie called to Mary over her shoulder.

"How about me?" Brian asked.

"Of course," his mother said, "but Mary first."

The staircase curved and ended at the second floor near the front windows. Annie led them to a door in the back of the hall. She opened it. "You first!" She made a sweeping gesture, indicating Mary should lead the way up a narrow dark staircase.

"What's this?" Mary stepped back.

"Go ahead. Go ahead," Annie insisted. "You'll see."

A cord dangled from a nail on the wall, and Mary yanked it.

"The electricity isn't on," her father said. "Just watch your step."

They had crowded in behind Mary, and she had no choice. She climbed the stairs and opened a small door at the top. The sudden light made her blink. The room was very bright. It was square, with two six-foot-tall windows set into each wall. She was in the room at the top of the house, Mary realized. It stood alone like an eagle's nest at the top of a tree.

"You're going to be our princess in the tower," Annie said. "What do you think of that?"

"I think I should love it. I mean, who wouldn't?"

"After all, you are fifteen. We thought you'd like some privacy." Her dad smiled at her expectantly. "Right?"

"Sure." Mary tried to sound enthusiastic.

"If Mary's going to be the princess, she has to grow her

4 ∽

hair. She needs hair like you, Ma," Brian said, pulling on his mother's long auburn braid.

"Why?" Annie asked.

"Wasn't that princess a prisoner in her tower? She had to let her hair down so the prince could climb up and rescue her."

"Oh." Annie laughed. "You're thinking of Rapunzel. I didn't mean that princess. I just meant Mary would be like royalty—mistress of all she surveyed."

"You've sure got the best views in Sound Port," her father said.

Mary followed him over to one of the windows that looked down on the back yard. In one corner stood a ramshackle green building. There were shingles missing from the roof, and a broken trellis had fallen by the door. "What's that?" Mary asked.

"A playhouse maybe," her father said.

Annie and Brian came over to look. "Or a summerhouse," Annie said. "But summerhouses were usually open, and this one has windows. I believe Victorian ladies used to lounge about in them in the summer heat."

"It's on fire!" Brian squeezed in front of Mary.

The windows glowed red: burning squares in the dark, decaying structure.

"That's just the sun setting," John Barrone said. "It's reflecting on the windows. They're not on fire."

The building had a ghostly look as if people had left it long ago and other tenants had moved in. Mary shook off that impression and surveyed the rest of the yard.

There had been gardens at one time, and still some phlox and black-eyed Susans struggled to bloom amid the weeds. A grape arbor sagged under leafless vines, and what had been lawn resembled a hayfield. The remains of a stone wall marked the boundaries of the yard. A dense wood grew close on three sides. It looked mysterious and forbidding.

"Come over here." John Barrone put his arm around Mary and steered her to a side window. "Isn't this great? We're surrounded by the Myanous Nature Preserve. That's the river in the distance."

"One of the owners gave a lot of land to the town, keeping only two acres and the house," Annie said. "Just imagine, we're only three miles from the center of the village, and you'd think we were somewhere in Vermont, for goodness' sake."

"And you have the best views in the place, Sam," her father repeated, calling her by the pet name he'd given her when she was little. "They'll be even better once I get the garden restored."

"I'm only marrying your father because he's in the landscape business, and I won't have to dig in the dirt," Annie joked. "Hey, we'd better move along, group. That sun's going down fast."

"I'll stay here a few minutes," Mary said. Annie was so cheery, it really got to her sometimes.

"To watch the sunset? I don't blame you." Her father patted her shoulder. "Come down before it gets too dark."

"Can I stay with Mary?" Brian asked.

6 ❧

Pull-eeze, Mary thought. She made a face, but didn't say anything.

"Don't you want to see your room?" Annie put her hand on Brian's shoulder and edged him to the stairs.

"I guess so," he said.

They were hardly out the door before Mary regretted her impulse, but she'd look dumb if she followed them. She squared her shoulders. The sun was now lighting up high clouds, and the sky looked as if some mad artist had wielded a paintbrush. The colors cast a lurid light on the landscape below.

She turned to the front windows that looked out over the lawn and the tree-enclosed driveway. Even from this height, she couldn't see the road.

If they bought this house, they'd really be alone back here. There were no neighbors. The gates to the nature preserve were a long way down the road. Her father had pointed them out as they drove by. Mary didn't understand why he and Annie thought it would be so neat to live out here in the boonies.

After all, when Mary and her father had left Freedom two years before and moved down here to Sound Port, he had said he was sick of the country, tired of a little one-horse town. She had loved Freedom and hadn't wanted to leave, but she wanted to please him. She knew he was lonely, that he missed her mother. But there was no use thinking about that now.

Mary turned to the last windows on the other side of the room. Nothing but trees, including a huge evergreen that partly covered the panes and disappeared from view at the top of one window. She wondered how long it had been growing.

The light was getting dim, the trees becoming shapes rather than distinct branches. She had better go down. Despite the open door to her room, the narrow stairway was dark. She put her hand on the wall to steady herself and carefully felt for each step.

Halfway down, there was a rustling under her hand. Mary jumped away, nearly losing her balance. She stopped, holding her breath. She listened. The sound came again: a scratching in the wall. It was almost like the rustle of paper. Like someone hiding in there crumpling up newspapers. A little gasp escaped her as she drew in breath.

The noise stopped.

Someone had heard her. Her neck prickled, and she hunched up her shoulders. She licked her lips. She slid her right foot forward, feeling for the edge of the stair. She let her foot slide over and down to the next tread. Carefully she drew her left foot down to the same stair, making no sound.

She waited a moment. It was still. Then she moved again, until she was two steps from the bottom. She was almost down when the door moved, slowly opening.

Mary could not hold back the scream.

Annie jumped back, her hand at her throat. "I'm sorry, honey," she said. "I didn't mean to startle you."

John Barrone and Brian came running down the hall. "What's going on?" her father asked.

"I scared her. I was just going to call her. I didn't know she was right there on the stairs."

"It wasn't that." Mary whispered, "I heard something in the wall." She looked over her shoulder, half expecting to see someone there.

"I'm not surprised. When people move out of a house, it isn't long before other creatures move in—especially in the walls. It was probably a mouse or a squirrel. We'll get an exterminator out here right away."

Her father sounded so calm and reasonable, Mary felt silly. A mouse or a squirrel. She had let her imagination run away with her. "Oh," she said, looking down at the floor.

"I was calling you because we have something special to ask you," Annie said. She bit her lip and opened her eyes wide like some little kid with a secret. "Let's go downstairs to *our* living room."

Our! So much for Brian's and my opinions of the house, Mary thought as she followed them downstairs. It sounded as if they were going to live here, like it or not.

When they were grouped in front of the fireplace, Annie said, "John. Go ahead."

John looked at Brian, who was standing in front of his mother, her hands on his shoulders. "Brian," he said, "I would like you to be my best man."

"Huh?" Brian looked up at his mother. "What does that mean? What would I have to do?"

"You'd be in charge of the rings," John answered.

"The justice of the peace—the man who's performing the ceremony—would tell you when to hand them to me. But the important part is you'd stand next to me and witness my marriage to your mother. The best man is usually the groom's best male friend. I hope that will be true of us. Think you can do it?"

"Yeah. I guess so. I hope I get that ring part right."

"You'll do just fine. Thank you, Brian," her father said seriously. He reached over and shook Brian's hand.

"My turn," Annie said, moving to Mary and taking her hand. Mary's hand lay cold and limp in Annie's warm grip. "Mary, I will be thrilled and delighted if you will be my maid of honor." Annie's eyes were bright and she blinked back tears.

Mary wanted to say, "No. No, I don't want to. Go ahead and marry Daddy, but don't make me a part of it." Instead, she pulled her hand away and looked at her father. "All right."

"*Won*-derful!" Annie acted as if Mary had been enthusiastic. "You know this wedding is for the four of us. We're all entering into a very special relationship. When the justice of the peace says, 'Do you take this man to be your lawfully wedded husband?' I want you kids to be thinking what it means to you. I hope Brian will be saying 'I do' right along with me. 'I do' join in and take this family to be my new family. And, Mary, when he asks your Dad, 'Do you take this woman,' I hope you'll find it in your heart to say yes as well."

Mary swallowed hard. The grownups were looking at

her eagerly. Her father's eyes beseeched her, willing her to speak.

"What do you think, Briny?" Annie finally turned to her son, and attention was mercifully diverted from Mary.

"Sounds kinda mushy to me." Brian made a face at his mother and laughed.

Annie and John laughed, too. "I'm afraid your poetry is lost on the young," John said.

It was too dark to explore any further. On the ride into town, Mary was quiet. In six weeks her father would be married, and they would move into that gloomy old house.

An image came into her mind. She was a little girl, and they were having a picnic by the river in Freedom. She was playing with a toy boat. She couldn't remember what happened, but suddenly the boat was floating away, and she couldn't reach it. It was turning and spinning in the current. She called her father, but when he got there, it was too late. The boat had gone too far. She had watched until it disappeared around a bend in the river.

That was the first time Daddy had ever failed her.

Chapter 2

" 'Lucid dreamers are able to fly without help, much like Superman—' " The beginning of Mary's oral report was interrupted by the laughter of some of the boys in her English class.

"I tried to fly like Superman when I was six years old," a blond, muscular boy in the back row offered. "Sprained my ankle jumping off the garage, flapping my arms."

"Where'd you land, Mike? On your head?" The dark-haired boy next to him punched Mike on the arm.

"That's enough flapping your mouths." Ms. Martinez pointed a finger at the young men. "This is very interesting. Go on, Mary."

Mary cleared her throat and looked down at the magazine article. " 'Lucid dreamers find flying an exciting way to travel,' " she read softly.

"First class or tourist?" Mike asked.

"That's enough, Mike," Ms. Martinez warned. "Mary, please explain what a lucid dreamer is. I've never heard the term."

"People who can control their dreams," Mary answered.

"How can they do that?" the teacher asked. "Most of us are at the mercy of what we saw that day—or ate for dinner. We have little to say about what we dream."

"The article explains that." Mary read on. " 'To make dream flight happen, repeat these words before you retire, "I will fly tonight." Then, picture the flight.' "

The jocks in the back row laughed again. "I'd like to see you fly, sweetheart," the dark-haired boy said in a stage whisper to Mike.

Ms. Martinez frowned and shook her head at the boys. "This is a scientific article. I want you to be serious. It's from *Science Today*, right, Mary?"

"Yes," Mary said. "Last month's issue."

The laughing boy raised his hand.

"Yes, Neil?"

"You gotta admit it sounds weird. Doesn't it, Ms. Martinez? Flying in your dreams. Gimme a break."

"And what's the point?" Mike joined in. "Why would you want to?"

"Mary, does the article address that question?" Ms. Martinez asked.

Mary shrugged. "Sort of. It's supposed to make the dreamer feel liberated, like really free. And if you get good at it, you're able to see the world from outer space. That's what it says, anyway."

"Can you only see what you already know?" a blond girl in the front row asked.

"Not according to this." Mary held up the magazine. "There's something called *dream spinning* where you can pick any person, any time period, and any place you want to visit. It doesn't even have to be real. You can pick a person or place in the past, present, or future."

"You mean I could visit, say, Shakespeare?" the blond girl asked.

Mary nodded.

"Or I could drop in on Jay Gatsby even though he was created by Fitzgerald and never existed?" Ms. Martinez asked.

"Right."

"That's an interesting idea," Ms. Martinez said. "Think about it, class. If you could go anywhere and visit anyone in your dreams, whom would you visit and when? Take a moment and jot down your answer."

It was quiet for a few seconds. Then Mike whispered something to Neil, and they both snickered.

"No X-rated trips," Ms. Martinez warned. "Respect the sensibilities of your middle-aged English teacher who was brought up before the revolution."

"Aw, come off it. You're not *that* old."

"The sexual revolution, Neil. Not the American Revolution." Ms. Martinez looked long-suffering, and the class roared.

Mary really liked Ms. Martinez. She knew how to joke around, but she also kept order.

"You have an answer, Jennifer?" The teacher called on the blond girl.

"Albert Einstein, because he was interested in time."

"Very good. Courtney?" She moved down the row.

"The Kentucky Derby. Any year. I love horses."

"Jody? What about you?"

"The Beatles at a concert in England in the sixties."

"Do I dare ask you, Mike?"

"Sure, Ms. Martinez. Darryl Strawberry: 1986 World Series, before he betrayed us."

The bell rang.

"Too bad," Ms. Martinez said. "Time's up. Your research led to a good discussion, Mary." She raised her hand, dismissing the class.

Mary sighed deeply. She was relieved it was over and it had turned out all right. She stood by the desk, waiting to speak to the teacher.

Ms. Martinez handed out assignments to the previous day's absentees, then turned to Mary. "Yes?"

"We have a major project for the quarter, right?" Mary asked. "I wondered if I could do some more research on dreams."

"That seems a little removed from literature," Ms. Martinez said. "How would you approach it?"

"Experiments have been done at Metropolitan State College. I thought I'd write for their results."

"Hmm. Firsthand sources. That appeals to me. Maybe we could justify it on the basis of research skills. It's nice to have a student realize that doing research does not mean copying from the encyclopedia."

"I thought I might try some of the experiments. They're described in the article, and there's a questionnaire to send in after you do them."

The teacher frowned slightly. "Do I have them?"

Mary pointed to the copy she had left on the teacher's desk before beginning her report. "There," she said.

Ms. Martinez picked it up. "For your oral assignments, it was 'anything goes.' I simply wanted to introduce the class to the media center and the various periodicals. A term project, you understand, has to be closely tied to English. I will look this over, however, and we'll discuss it on Monday." She gave a little wave, dismissing Mary. "See you then."

Adults always had reservations, Mary thought—even Ms. Martinez, who seemed so broad-minded and open. English was Mary's favorite class, though. The kids seemed friendlier than in most of her other classes at the high school.

Mary had been in eighth grade when they moved to Connecticut. Moving had been really hard. She had known everyone in Freedom. She knew no one in Sound Port. There had been 16 kids in her class in upstate New York. Here there were 160 in eighth grade, so it was no wonder there were cliques. She had tried, had done stuff like working on the yearbook. That had been okay, but once the meetings were over, she had always found herself on her own.

Now she was a sophomore at the high school. Students were from three public junior highs and from several private schools. There were nearly two thousand, double the entire population of Freedom.

Going home, Mary sat alone on the school bus. Most of the kids got off long before her road. She read again the article on dreams and studied the exercises. There were two sets: one that described dream flying and one that gave instructions for dream spinning.

The idea of moving around in time and space fascinated Mary. Being able to control her dreams really appealed to her. Last night she'd had a bad dream, probably because she was nervous about giving her report. She dreamed the teacher had called on her, and she couldn't find her homework. She had looked through her notebook, had run to her locker. But there was no locker. Instead there were piles of cardboard cartons that she couldn't open. Mary had woken up, her heart pounding. She hated dreams like that.

After her mother had died, she had dreamed about her. Waking up had been unbearable. Mary felt her throat tighten, and it was hard to swallow. Those were the worst dreams.

She looked again at the article, willing herself to concentrate. Lucid dreamers were in charge. Their dreams were exciting, adventurous, happy. They could go in and out of them at will.

Mary was startled when the bus driver leaned over and touched her arm. "Isn't this your stop?" he asked.

"Oh!" Mary jumped up.

"A million miles away," he teased. "Probably thinking about the party you're going to this weekend."

Mary didn't answer. She just looked down as he pushed the lever, and the door wheezed open. Then she jumped from the step to the ground.

The bus had let her off at Lockwood Lane, a narrow, twisting road often wide enough for only one car at a time. At this end of the street there were some houses. They were far apart and set back. Mary caught glimpses of them down driveways or past hedges. It was a clear October day. The leaves had turned, and the brilliant oranges of the maples shone in the sun.

A fifteen-minute walk brought her to the large pillars at the main entrance of the Myanous Nature Preserve. For the remaining half mile there were woods on both sides of the road. Except for an occasional squirrel running up a tree or the rustle of some small animal in the brush, Mary was alone.

She was glad to get to her driveway. The trees that lined it had turned yellow since she had first been there two months before. Some leaves had fallen, making it golden, like the highway to Oz.

The house had been freshly painted, and Mary had to admit that it looked much better. Broken panes of glass had been replaced, and an exterminator had rid the walls of their former inhabitants.

Mary walked up the front steps and looked through the glass at the big, empty front hall. The door was unlocked, and she opened it. "Anyone home?" she called, going inside.

Her voice sounded hollow in the empty rooms. No one answered. Drop cloths were spread around the living and dining rooms, and there was an odd packing box here and there. Mary's footsteps were loud on the hardwood floors.

The kitchen was an improvement. The old cabinets had been refinished, and some new ones with glass doors installed. The white-and-green tile floor was bright and cheerful. Windows across the back let in a lot of light. Mary helped herself to an apple from a bowl on the counter and stood irresolutely looking out into the yard.

Annie had probably gone to pick up Brian at the grammar school. He got out an hour after Mary. Annie often arranged to be finished at her real estate office just before Brian's school was over, Mary had noticed. He hardly ever had to take the bus and walk the length of Lockwood Lane.

Better get at her unpacking, she decided. They had been in the house a week, and she hadn't made a dent in the boxes. She had some she'd brought from Freedom and never opened in the small apartment her father had rented.

Mary went back to the front hall and up the staircase to the second floor. She opened the door that led to her room, pulling on the chain that was strung along the wall from the top to the bottom of the stairwell. It lit a bare lightbulb that swung from the ceiling. The third step let out a squeak that sounded loud in the empty house.

She hurried up the stairs and through the door at the top. She was learning to like her room, especially on a day like this when light poured in the eight windows. Mary walked over and opened the back windows a few inches. The room was quite warm.

The woods, except for the evergreens, had turned brilliant fall colors. It made them less forbidding. But the summerhouse, slumped in a corner of the yard, made her uneasy. She had hoped her father would have it torn down.

It was a relief to turn back to her room, which definitely needed work. The wallpaper was a faded rose pattern and peeling in places. Annie had been after her to pick out new paper, but she hadn't gotten around to it. Mary didn't know why her stepmother thought it would be such a fun project for the two of them. Mary doubted if she would be any good at wallpapering. It was just another of Annie's schemes to make them a family.

"Hello—oo . . ." Annie's cheerful voice drifted up the stairs. "We're ho—ome."

"Mary, Mary, quite contrary," Brian chanted as he clattered up the stairs to the second floor. "Come on down, Mary."

"I'm unpacking," Mary called back.

"Can I come up?" Brian asked from the bottom of her stairs.

"Leave Mary alone now, Brian," his mother said.

That saved her answering, Mary thought, as she looked around wondering where to begin. There were shelves on one wall, and she decided to unpack a carton of books. She cut the cord on a large box. The first six she pulled out were Nancy Drew mysteries, and she had to laugh at herself for hanging on to them. Though they were all written to formula, there were scenes she still remembered, like the creepiness of Nancy hearing the click of high heels in an old house before a storm. But no matter the danger, Nancy always triumphed. Mary liked that surety, and she had reread each book again and again.

She put Nancy on the shelf and pulled out her baseball books. That was another passion—especially the Mets. One of the better parts of living in Connecticut had been going to Shea Stadium with her father, before he'd gotten so busy with his wedding and working on the house.

The third stair creaked. "Can I come up?" It was Brian.

"I suppose so," Mary said reluctantly.

"You putting your books away?" Brian walked over to the shelf. "Hey, this looks good. Can I borrow it?" He held up *The Secret of the Old Clock*.

"Sure. I think I was about your age when I started reading Nancy Drew."

"Can I stay here and read?" Brian sat down on the bed.

"Not a good idea," Mary said. "I have a lot to do, and I'll need the bed to spread stuff out. You can take the book, though."

"Don't be contrary, Mary," he wheedled.

"Brian, I'm busy. I really am."

"Busy, dizzy. Can I just stay until you finish that box?"

"All right." Mary sighed.

There was no getting rid of Brian. When she finished the first box and started making piles on the bed, he slid down on the floor. "I'm not in the way here," he said.

Mary was reading a paper she had written in second grade when suddenly Brian snorted and laughed. "Boy, you didn't win any prizes in art, did you?"

Mary looked over. "Give me that," she said angrily, "and stay out of my stuff!" She snatched the faded manila page from him. "Now go away!"

"I didn't do anything," he whined.

"I'll call your mother."

"Okay. Okay." He stuck out his tongue at her as he got up. Then he left, slamming the door.

Mary looked down at the paper in her hand. There were three stick figures: a tall one drawn in black, a smaller one in red, and between them a tiny yellow child. All three were smiling, and rays circled their heads, making the picture joyful. Mary had drawn it in first grade. There was the title, *My Family*.

She put it away quickly as old, angry feelings came flooding back. Brian was a pest, and she had never been crazy about Annie, who seemed as different from her quiet, petite mother as a woman could be. They would never belong in a picture of Mary's family, no matter how hard her father tried.

Mary slumped on her bed. The sun had gone down,

and darkness pressed against all eight windows. Suddenly it seemed cold in the room, and the light Brian had turned on to read by hardly dispelled the feeling that she was completely alone, separated from the people below by more than a single story.

Mary brooded through dinner. The minute her father finished his last forkful, she asked to be excused.

"Since there's no cable out here and lousy TV reception, I thought we might play Scrabble tonight," John Barrone said.

"I have homework," Mary answered.

"On Friday night?" He looked disappointed. "Can't you do it over the weekend?"

"It's a really important term project, and I have to get started." Mary stood up.

"I think it's *wonderful*"—Annie had a way of lingering on a word every so often, drawing it out, exaggerating it, that irked Mary—"that a fifteen-year-old girl is a serious student."

"But all work and no play—" her father protested.

Mary leaned down and kissed his cheek. "See you later."

Homework had been an excuse, but Mary decided she would write to Metropolitan State College for case studies of its experiments with lucid dreamers. She set up her typewriter and looked at *Science Today* to get the necessary information. In the letter she expressed interest in taking part in the experiments.

When she had finished, she looked at the exercises.

The article said dream flying was easy to master. She was tempted to try it.

It sounded simple. All she had to do was keep repeating, "I will fly tonight," and picture herself flying. So why not?

She turned out the desk light.

She stood by the window and stared out into the night. A full moon illuminated the back yard. She could see the dark line of the wall, but could not make out individual stones. A leaf, robbed of its color by the moon, twirled past the glass. The summerhouse was a dark shape in the whitened landscape. Mary gazed a long time. The night was hypnotic.

She had made up her mind. She crossed the room, bright in the moonlight, and lay down on her bed. "I will fly tonight," she said aloud.

Was it really possible? she wondered.

She closed her eyes. She must picture herself floating. She could do it. She would do it. See herself floating above the bed.

"I will fly tonight," she said again. "Oh, yes, tonight I will fly. Tonight I will fly." She imagined her body, weightless, suspended in the moonlight.

Suspended in the moonlight.

Suspended . . . in the light of the moon.

The pale white light bathed the earth in brightness.

Mary felt that she was drifting, that she had left behind that which was solid. As if she had left a shore and floated on a sea of moonlight.

She was outside and light as the moon-filled air.

Objects below were clear but without detail. The soft air embraced her, slowing her descent. Her feet touched the dewy ground, and she was walking, weightless, walking to the summerhouse. The trees cast long shadows that shifted on the ground as a breeze blew the branches above. The summerhouse was whole, unbroken, straight. Its windows glinted in the light of the moon. On its trellised vines, miraculously restored, a single flower bloomed.

Mary's step was light, and she rose above the ground. She was drawn to the darkness of the woods behind the stone wall. Her shadow floated with her, a darkness drawn to darkness. She felt the cold stones under her feet as she balanced on the wall. She wavered and felt she would fall. She put her hand out to the moonlit air to catch herself and lifted off the stones to balance once more in the air above them.

She rose higher and higher until she was flying above the forest. It was clear and pale and white in the moonlight. There were shadowy paths, and in the trees she could see the night creatures: the pale yellow eyes of a raccoon, the horned head of an owl, hunched over, seeking its prey. Then a fair, soft-colored fawn danced along a path, drawn like her to some mystery. Enchanted, she followed the fawn, sometimes part of shadows, sometimes shining in the gleam of moonlit patches. It drew her to the river, silvery surface over dark depths, making no noise, though it moved and shimmered between its banks. The fawn stopped and sniffed the night air, fragrant with the smell of burning apple wood and hickory. It stood poised, quiet, then seemed to slide away into the forest. A flick of a white tail, and it was gone.

Chapter 3

Rain splattered against her windows, half waking Mary in the morning. She lay there while the sounds of the rain faded in and out of her consciousness, trying to recapture the dream of the night before. Images came and went—the moon-washed forest, the trusting deer. She had really felt the absence of weight, of fear, of earthbound troubles. Mary had never been so free, joined in some mystical way with nature while her body lay asleep. She was filled with yearning and burrowed deeper into the covers, determined not to let the dream escape.

But it wouldn't come back, and the rain grew louder. Muffled noises from the second floor mixed with sounds from outside. The family was getting up.

Mary stumbled out of bed and over to the window.

The rain-swept back yard surprised her. Yellowed grass, rearranged by the light storm, was bent and flattened. The crumbling stone wall made a haphazard line. The summerhouse looked a beaten thing. Nothing was as it had been in her dream. Yet she had flown above this yard, of that she was certain. Perhaps in another time.

The rain continued all weekend, keeping them indoors. In the middle of unpacking a box or holding a T square for her father, Mary found herself staring off into space, returning to the dream and feeling a curious sense of loss.

Brian and her father were eating, and Annie was pouring coffee when Mary hurried in to breakfast on Monday morning. Mary always anticipated her first look at her stepmother, whose outfits could be counted on to wake anyone up. Today, in a striped black-and-yellow jersey dress, Annie resembled a large bumblebee.

Simple breakfasts had always been good enough for the two of them when Mary and her father had been alone. Since the marriage, or THE MARRIAGE, which was the way Mary thought of it, John Barrone had made a production of breakfast, even on weekdays. This Monday morning there was a big platter of French toast and a pitcher of syrup on the table.

The sun shone in the large set of windows that formed a nook for the breakfast table. The grownups sat at either end, and she and Brian faced the back yard. The day looked bright and inviting after the dreary weekend.

As they were exchanging good mornings, the telephone rang. Annie plucked the cordless phone from the wall. "Annie Barrone here," she said. There was a pause. "B-a-r-r-o-n-e," she spelled. "Barrone. Rhymes with macaroni." Annie laughed.

Mary winced. Annie thought she was *so* funny.

"Yes. You have the right number. I've remarried, and my name has changed, but my number hasn't. You want Brian?" She held out the phone. "It's for you, Briny."

"Yeah?" Brian spoke into the receiver.

"Is that the way he answers the telephone? Yeah?" Mary's father raised his eyebrows.

"I'll ask my mother." Brian put his hand over the receiver. "Can I go to Sharon's after school? Her mom'll bring me home."

"Yes, if you're here by six," Annie said. She ignored her husband's question.

"See ya at school." Brian handed Annie the phone. "We're gonna work on her dollhouse. Want to see the kitchen table I made her?" He pushed back from the table and jumped out of his chair.

"Sit down until you finish your breakfast," John Barrone said.

"Yes, love, finish your French toast. Then you can show us. Brian is so good with his hands. He's practically furnished his little friend's dollhouse."

"Dollhouse furniture?" It was clear that John didn't approve.

"I'd love to see it," Mary said. "I never had a dollhouse, but I always wanted one."

"Can I go get it? Huh? Can I?"

"Two more bites," Annie said. "You know how important it is that you eat balanced meals and that you eat enough. You don't want to have an insulin reaction in school."

"Ma—aa!" Brian turned red and glared at his mother.

"I love family breakfasts," Annie went right on. "They just start the day off right. I mean, not only are they good nutritionally speaking, but they give us a structure. And you make great French toast, John." She looked at Brian, who was chewing the last of a large mouthful. "You may be excused, Briny."

"He has an awful lot of girlfriends, doesn't he?" Mary's father asked, once Brian had left the room.

Annie laughed. "Wait until he's sixteen," she said. "Some of these kids are little beauties."

"When I was his age, I didn't give girls the time of day."

"We lived in a neighborhood where there were mostly little girls," Annie said. "They've been his friends since he was a toddler. I don't think it's anything to worry about."

"See what I made." Brian came into the kitchen and went right to Mary. He handed her a miniature table that he had built of twigs, fastened together with rawhide laces.

"It's really good," Mary said.

Annie held out her hand, and Mary passed her the table. "Wow, Briny," Annie said. "I've seen big tables like this at craft shows. They cost a fortune."

"This is very good, Brian." His stepfather took the

little table from Annie. "I think you should try your hand at bigger projects. Maybe you could make a full-sized table, as your mother suggests."

"Naw," said Brian. "I like making little stuff."

"We'd better get going." Mary looked at the clock on the kitchen shelf, which read 7:30.

"I'll give you a ride to the bus stop this morning. I have to meet a client on the other side of town at eight." Her father rose and picked up his suit jacket from the back of his chair.

Mary stuffed the letter to the university in her book bag. She would have Ms. Martinez look it over after class.

They did not have assigned seats in English. Mary always tried to find a place in the middle and on one side. She did not want to sit in front, where she would be called on, or in back, where the jocks sat.

After attendance, Ms. Martinez announced that she wanted them to work with partners. It was a relief when the teacher said she would assign them. It was a relief until she called Mary's name and paired it with Mike Bell. He was one of the guys from the back row. He was good-looking and sure of himself. Although only a sophomore, he was one of the stars of the swim team.

Mary didn't know if she was supposed to go and sit with him, or if he would come up and sit with her. She was too embarrassed to turn around. She reached into her bag and pulled out her notebook. It gave her something to do.

"Hi, partner." Two large hands appeared on her desk,

and she looked up to see him leaning down, grinning at her. "Who's your hero?" he asked.

That was the assignment. They were preparing to read *The Odyssey*, and they were supposed to come up with a definition of a hero.

"I . . . I don't know." Her mind was a total blank.

Mike pulled a chair up next to her, scraping it across the floor. "What about John F. Kennedy? My dad thinks he was the greatest."

"Oh, mine, too." Mary was grateful he'd started the discussion. "My father also admired Martin Luther King." She had managed to come up with a name.

"Why don't you write them down?" Mike suggested. Mary realized she was still clutching the notebook. She dropped it on the desk, then opened it to a blank page. Mike took a pen from his shirt pocket and handed it to her. She wrote the two names on the first and second lines.

"Boy, do you write small!" Mike said.

"Maybe you want to . . . ?" She held out the pen.

"Naw. That's okay. Your handwriting's pretty—all neat and even. So, let's see. Who else would we put down? How about somebody like Jackie Robinson? He was out there on the front line when being black in baseball was rough."

Mary nodded and added the name. "What about the Amazing Mets?" She surprised herself with the question.

Mike laughed. "How do you know about them?"

"I've been a fan since I was really young," Mary said.

"Me too. We'll have to compare notes someday. I don't think they make the list, though, do you?"

"I was only kidding."

"There'd be lots of presidents. Like Jefferson. I visited Monticello once. You know? His mansion. It was loaded with his inventions."

"Didn't he write the Declaration of Independence?"

"Sounds right. So put him down. Can you think of anyone from a different field? Anyone from today?"

"Maybe Mother Teresa?"

"Good one," Mike agreed. "And that shows a hero can be male or female. Make a note of it for our definition."

Mary was surprised that Mike was taking the assignment so seriously. She had thought he would be the type to fool around. She started to relax.

"What about some of the people who have given concerts to help others?"

"Right. Like world hunger and AIDS. Plenty of groups have gone all out. But they're not individuals. Can a group be a hero?"

They debated that, but had to agree that all the people who fought Hitler in World War II were heroes. They were adding names and groups to their list when Ms. Martinez announced she would call for definitions in five minutes.

They studied the list.

"I got it," Mike said.

"What?"

"These people all changed the world in some way."

"For the better," Mary added.

"Right on! Hey, we're a good team, partner." Mike nudged her. "Maybe we'll work together another time."

Mary picked up his pen. "I'd better write down that definition."

The teacher singled them out to compliment. Mike took her hand and held it aloft with his in a sign of victory. She was embarrassed, but it was worth it.

"Let's go into the learning center," Ms. Martinez said to Mary after class. "I want to talk to you about your project."

The learning center was a workroom for teachers and a place for students to get help in English or social studies. At one small table an instructional aide was helping a student with her essay. A boy was making up a test at another table. Bookcases screened Ms. Martinez's desk from the rest of the room.

"Here's the letter I've written to the university," Mary said, handing it to the teacher.

Ms. Martinez scanned it quickly. "I have real problems with this," she said.

"What?" Mary was taken by surprise.

"I read through the article. Certainly it's a reputable magazine and a respected university doing the experiments, but I'm just not comfortable with certain aspects."

"I don't understand," Mary said.

"The purpose of the article seems to be to attract volunteers for these dream experiments. But the volunteers aren't monitored. Scientific experiments should take place in a laboratory under close supervision. I don't want you taking part in it. Not under the aegis of the English department. It sounds uncontrolled and risky."

"Risky?" Mary's voice echoed her disbelief.

"The article promises you the world in your dreams: 'Meet your Prince Charming'; 'Take part in *Star Wars.*' It's seductive. That kind of dreaming, if one could really master it, could become an escape."

The dream came back into Mary's mind. Those wonderful sensations of floating and flying . . .

"Mary? You have a faraway look in your eye. Do you understand my objections?"

Mary blinked. "No. Not really."

"Let me just say that I would not do those experiments, and I don't want you to. You may rewrite the letter if you like and simply ask for case studies. You really need to tie it in to literature in some way."

"I don't see how." Mary did not try to hide her disappointment.

"Perhaps some of the subjects have used their dreams in writing. Mary Shelley, for example, got the idea for *Frankenstein* in a dream—actually, a nightmare. You might ask."

When Mary didn't answer, the teacher made another suggestion. "Maybe you'll find some common ground in the people who do get involved, or perhaps you could write a short story based on a case study."

"Maybe."

"Don't be discouraged." Ms. Martinez patted her hand. "You are an intelligent young lady. You'll find an

interesting way to use the research. Just no experiment-
ing."

Mary thought about their conversation all week. Ms.
Martinez had been really emphatic when she had for-
bidden her to dream. As if Mary would try to meet some
Prince Charming! That was silly. Of course, Mary knew
she could dream anytime she wanted to. It really wasn't
any of Ms. Martinez's business what she did apart from
English class. She liked the teacher a lot, though, and
respected her opinion. She argued with herself every
night.

On Friday night the moon was lower in the sky, and
smaller. It formed a path of light from the back windows
across the floor and onto Mary's bed.

As yet, the windows had no curtains. Mary felt surrounded and enveloped by the night, and the path beckoned in the waning moonlight. She was unable to resist,
and like an incantation, she repeated the words, "I will
fly tonight." Over and over she said them until once
more she was out there, floating light as the very air
around her. And the dream possessed her.

*The three-quarter moon was ghostly white in the night
sky, but no stars shone. Its light illuminated the summerhouse, and from the cottage came a melody played on a
piano. Tinkling notes danced on the night air and disappeared. Again the stone wall stood with every stone in
place, and beyond it the forest.*

A silvery path beckoned. Mary followed it to a large

meadow dotted with juniper bushes, their blue berries turned black in the pale light. Beyond the meadow, a shallow brook flowed over a rocky bottom. In the distance there was a rumbling that might have been thunder.

Mary felt herself borne higher. The brook gathered speed and depth. She followed it until, cascading over a steep bank, it emptied into the river. Here the river was wide and moving swiftly. To her right and set back from the riverbank, a clapboard building formed a dark square in a clearing. Mary descended. A sign on its peaked roof was barely distinguishable. RIVERVIEW, it read. A wooden awning covered a platform on all sides of the building. In front ran a double row of railroad tracks. Beyond, the river was a dull, metallic glow, patched by shadows of overhanging branches. Over the river stood a wooden bridge with a barnlike structure covering the center.

Next to the building was an open buggy, its spoked back wheels larger than the front wheels. Two benches with curved leather back rails sat on its wooden platform. A horse stood motionless between two narrow wooden poles attached to his harness.

The station seemed to be deserted, but as Mary watched, a pale light could be seen through the station window. She became conscious of a faint, low hum in the distance, a sound that was more vibration than noise. The railroad tracks gleamed silver and seemed to glow brighter as the hum rose in pitch. Nothing moved, but the night was charged with the energy of the approaching train. When it appeared, a round, yellowish light seemed to float bodiless

36 ᧐

through the woods above the silver tracks, turning them to a faint gold.

Clickety-clack, clickety-clack, whoosh, whoosh; clickety, clickety, clickety, and with a sigh, the piston-driven wheels, clear now in the moonlight, slid to a stop in a cloud of foggy steam.

Mary was waiting for someone to emerge, but no one came. It was as if time had stopped and she was looking at a picture: the stilled train, the unmoving horse and buggy, the dark station with its one feeble light. Where were the people?

Then whiter steam puffed from the stack behind the lantern. Slowly the wheels began to turn, and the train moved out of the station. Mary watched as it chugged toward the river and the covered bridge.

Over the sound of the wheels rose the loud, wailing, drawn-out call of the steam whistle, which seemed to moan and mourn, casting a pall over the scene. Then it was gone, and with it, the moon disappeared, and Mary was left alone, in darkness.

Chapter 4

~~~~~~

Mary stood staring out the window at the over-grown back yard. She did not remember waking up and getting out of bed. She leaned her forehead against the cold glass and shut her eyes against the ugliness.

She tried to remember the melody that had come from the summerhouse, but the tune eluded her. It had been sweet and delicate, part of the moonlit magic. It was the distant music of the past.

That was what had occurred. She had flown back to another time—a time of horses and steam engines and candlelight. An era when Sound Port had been called Riverview.

Mary did not know how it had happened. She had not willed it. She had simply chosen to fly. What had drawn her, then? What force had called her to that station in the night to hear that train? She shivered and pulled back from the window.

She told herself to stop being silly. After all, it was only a dream. Yet . . .

Resolutely she opened the door and plodded down the narrow stairway. In the bathroom she shared with Brian, towels lay in a heap on the floor, and there were a used cotton ball and syringe on the sink. She shuddered, thinking of Brian giving himself shots for his diabetes. Gingerly she picked up the needle and cotton, using a washcloth so she wouldn't have to touch them, and dropped them in the wastebasket.

Mary ran the water and stepped into the warm spray. She rubbed shampoo in her hair and turned the water on full force, letting it rain down hard on her face and head. When she got downstairs, her father was sanding a doorway in the living room. His dark, curly hair was covered with fine powder, making him look gray. "Hi, Sam," he said, reaching out with his free hand and pulling her over to kiss her cheek.

"Morning, Daddy."

"Look at this." He let her go and ran his hand lovingly over the woodwork. "Beautiful carved wood under these layers of paint."

"There you are. Oh, good." Annie appeared in the doorway. She was wearing green paisley jodhpur-like slacks that drew attention to her plump figure. Her hair was braided and wound around her head. "You're the last one up. I've saved you some pancakes."

"Thanks anyway," Mary said. "I just want juice and coffee."

"That's a terrible way to start the day," her father said. "You have some pancakes."

"Don't nag her, John." Annie shook a finger at him. "You fix her a good breakfast every morning. Let Mary suit herself over the weekend. Brian loves pancakes. He'll eat the leftovers for lunch."

"Where is Brian? I thought he might give me a hand with this sanding."

"He's got his nose in a book Mary lent him. You are a *won*-derful influence, big sister!"

"Oh." Her father smiled approvingly. "Getting your brother reading, are you?"

"I'm not getting *Brian* reading." Mary wished they wouldn't rush this family bit. He was not her brother. "I lent him a couple of Nancy Drew books, is all. It's no big deal."

"Nancy Drew?" He frowned. "Why'd you give him girls' books?"

When Mary didn't answer, he said, "Well, tell him I could use some help."

Annie followed Mary into the kitchen, chattering away, while Mary got her breakfast. "How'd you sleep? I love the autumn for sleeping. In the summer I sweat and slide around in the sheets." She pulled a platter of pancakes out of the oven. "Maybe just one?"

Mary shook her head. She knew Annie would keep talking without an answer.

"Brian will eat yours," Annie said, putting them down

on the stove. "Poor kid can't have many treats." She took a seat at the counter by Mary. "You've made a real hit with him. I didn't marry your father to get Brian a sister, but I'm glad it's worked out that way." Mary marveled at the way Annie jumped from one thought to another. "Brian's had a raw deal. No father. Of course, that's not literally true. It wasn't the immaculate conception. His father's out in Oregon, you know."

Mary didn't know. Backgrounds had not been given in an orderly fashion. Mary picked up information as it dropped haphazardly from Annie's mouth.

"Once he flew Brian out there for a week. But since Brian has been diabetic, no way."

Brian's disease had been discussed very little. Mary was both curious and repelled—especially disgusted when he forget to throw his stuff away, as he had this morning, "How did he get it?" she asked.

"It's inherited. My ex had a great-uncle who was diabetic, though you'd think it was my fault, to hear him tell it. And I don't know who Brian blames. Everybody, I guess. He's angry, and you can see why. He hates to talk about it. I worry about the psychological—" Annie stopped abruptly. "I didn't mean to get started on this. You've hardly had a chance to wake up."

"It's all right," Mary said. "I've wondered about it. When did he get sick?"

"Two years ago, when he was eight." Annie's expression grew serious, sadder than Mary had ever seen her look. "He got thin as a rail. It was pitiful. He urinated dozens of times a day, it seemed. They put him in the hospital to regulate the insulin. He isn't one of the lucky ones who can just take pills. He has to give himself shots. It breaks my heart."

The back door opened and Brian came in. Annie put a finger to her lips. It wasn't necessary. Mary was not going to ask any more questions.

Brian held up the book she had lent him. "This was great. Can I borrow another one?"

"You finished the second one already?" Mary asked.

"They aren't long."

"I have a lot more. You can come up later and pick out another."

"What are you doing today, Mary?"

"I'm going for a walk."

"My goodness," Annie said. "You certainly sound emphatic. Where are you going?"

"Just out back. Out in the woods." Mary had made up her mind. She was going to check out her dreams. She would see if there was a path or a meadow or a brook that led to the river. There might even be a station. She doubted it. It was really hard to imagine in the daytime.

"Can I come? Huh? Can I come?" Brian pleaded.

Mary hesitated. She had wanted to go alone. But what was the harm if Brian came? "I guess so," she said.

"Sir John wants you to help with the sanding, Brian," Annie said.

Right after the wedding, the four of them had discussed what the children would call their new stepparents. Annie had first suggested "Mother Anne," but quickly rejected it, saying it made her sound like a nun. Mary had settled on just plain "Annie," but rarely called her stepmother by any name.

"What do you want me to call you?" Brian had asked his stepfather.

"You could start with 'sir.' " John Barrone had meant it as a joke, but Brian had latched on to it. He had called him "Sir John" from then on, and Annie had picked it up as well.

"Sanding. Yick." Brian wrinkled his nose.

"Not yick. We all have to pitch in," Annie said, "but I'll make a deal with you. Go with Mary now, and give Sir John an hour or two this afternoon. Okay?"

He made a face. "If I have to."

"Here." Annie handed him an apple, then explained to Mary, "Brian has to carry food with him. If he gets hungry, he could have an insulin reaction."

"Mom! Don't!"

"Mary has to know about these things, Briny. She hasn't had any experience with dia—"

"Just be quiet. Okay? I can take care of myself." Brian's face was red.

"I'll take an apple, too," Mary said quickly. Their jackets were hanging on hooks in the back hall. She gave Brian his and put hers on, then stuffed her apple in the pocket.

"Have fun, children, and be back by noon," Annie called as they went down the back steps.

Mary looked at the old stone wall, trying to gauge just

where the moonlit path had been. She settled on an area to the left of the summerhouse. The trees did not look as dense, and the underbrush looked passable.

She led the way. In some places, they had to bend almost double and hold back tree branches. In others, there was little growth, and it was easy walking. Either way, they were hemmed in by woods that bore no resemblance to those in Mary's dream.

The forest was brilliant. Oranges, yellows, and reds contrasted with the evergreens. When they came out into a clearing, Mary looked for low, spreading juniper. Instead, she saw only pine and spruce. Yet there was something familiar about the grove.

Brian climbed up on a large rock and sprawled at the top. "How far do you think we've come?"

"Maybe a mile. It seemed longer because we had to make our own path."

"Do you think we ought to go back?"

"Why? You tired, Brian?"

"Naw. I just wondered if we could get lost."

"Not with the sun out. But if you want to go back, I'll take you."

"It's okay. I'll keep going."

Mary took off the bandanna that was wound around her head and tied it to a tree branch at the entrance of the path they had made. "It's easy to get turned around in the woods," she told Brian. "If we come back here, we'll know the way home."

Across the clearing, Mary spotted an opening in the

woods and a narrow trail. "Looks like animals made this," she said. "Let's go this way."

It was fairly easy walking, and they climbed over the odd branch or tree across their path. After ten minutes, Mary stopped. "Listen. You hear that?"

"What?"

She smiled. "Water. That's why the animals made this trail."

They skirted the edge of a large boulder. Around it, Mary found herself on the bank of a brook. On the other side, no more than five feet away, stood a deer. Mary could see water dripping from its chin. It was looking right at her, ears raised. Involuntarily, she drew in a breath. There had been a deer in her first dream.

There was a sound behind her, and she put a hand back in warning to Brian. She felt him stop moving, and she grabbed his sleeve, pulling him up next to her.

"Wow!" he said.

"Shhhh!"

But the spell was broken. The deer wheeled and bounded off into the woods. There was a flicker of its white tail. Then, crashing through the brush, it disappeared.

"That's the first deer I've ever seen," Brian said. "Except in a zoo."

Mary stood gazing at the spot where the deer had been.

"Must be your first one, too." Brian tugged at her sleeve.

"No." Mary shook her head.

"Then why're you looking so funny?" He peered up at her face.

"Because—because—I've never been so close to one before." Especially one that I saw in a dream, she thought. Brian was still staring at her. She pulled away from him.

"I saw lots of deer when we lived in the country." Mary was determined to sound rational. "I'd see them in the morning on my way to school. Sometimes they'd be right in the pastures with cows." There really was nothing special about seeing a deer, she argued with herself.

"That musta been neat," Brian said. "Hey." He pointed at the brook. "Should we try to get across?"

Mary looked down at the water. If the brook led to the river, her dreams would have a certain reality. It was all very well to dismiss the deer; it would be quite another thing to pooh-pooh a train station. She had to know. She would follow this brook. There was less brush on the other bank, which would make walking easier.

"Come this way," she told Brian. A few yards downstream, the brook was shallow. Large rocks protruded above the water. Mary stepped on one rock, then a second. She held her hand out to Brian. They moved from stone to stone. Brian slipped once and almost lost his footing, but Mary had a tight grip on his arm and kept him from falling.

Once on the other side, they picked up their pace. The sun got higher in the sky and warmed up the day.

They tied their jackets around their waists, and their collars grew damp with sweat.

"I'd better eat my apple," Brian said.

"You okay?"

"Yeah. I just need to eat something. I'm—hungry."

They sat under a tree while Brian ate. Mary was getting a little worried. She wished they hadn't walked so far, or that she hadn't let Brian come with her. She should have gotten a map of the preserve instead of relying on her dream.

She had better give it up for today. They were going deeper into the woods and there was no sign of the river, much less a train station.

She had a good sense of direction. If they walked toward the east, they would be heading for the main gate of the preserve. They might even come upon a trail.

They started off again in the new direction. Mary kept glancing back at Brian. She could see sweat on his forehead. She tried to remember Annie's warning before they left. Something about an insulin reaction.

"How you doing?" she asked.

"All right." Brian wiped his forehead with his sleeve.

She wanted to ask what would happen if he had a reaction, but Annie had said he hated to talk about it. Mary remembered now miserable he'd looked when his mother tried to caution them.

"You sure you're okay?"

"Yes," he said loudly.

"Here," Mary said, handing him her apple. "I don't want this. You eat it."

↬ 47

He hesitated, and Mary was afraid he was going to refuse. Then he took it and stuffed it into his pocket. "I'll have it later, maybe." His lower lip stuck out defiantly.

They kept going, Mary in the lead. They reached a stand of evergreens, tall pine trees, their lowest branches high off the ground. The carpet of needles was soft underfoot.

"It—smells—good. Like—Christmas," Brian said, sucking in air between each word.

Mary looked at him. She was sure he was sweating more. She wished he would eat the apple. "Brian?"

"Huh?"

"Never mind." It would do no good to push him.

He was lagging, though, slowing down. Mary thought about turning around, retracing their steps. But going back the way they had come would take too long. He might pass out or something. She bit her lip.

"Can you go a little faster?" Mary asked. "We can't be far from the main gate." This was more of a prayer than a statement.

"Uh-huh," he said. His breathing was loud. He was obviously tired.

They came to the top of a rise. Below, she caught sight of something red through the trees. She ran down the slope, Brian behind her.

Chapter 5

∾∾∾∾∾∾∾∾∾∾∾∾∾∾∾∾∾∾

Mary had caught sight of a red jacket, and the boy wearing it turned out to be Mike Bell, her partner in English class.

"Am I glad to see you!" she blurted.

"Hey, I'm always glad to see you, Mary Barrone." He grinned, and his whole face crinkled.

Brian came up beside her, panting. "We were lost!"

"Not exactly lost." Mary was embarrassed.

"Then you must have been glad to see me for some other reason," Mike teased.

Mary felt her face go red. "We were looking for a marked trail."

"You're on one now." Mike pointed to a yellow wooden square nailed to a tree. "See the marker? There are several to guide you. Follow them about a quarter of a mile, and you'll come out at the main gate. I'll walk back with you."

Only a quarter of a mile. Mary sighed with relief.

Brian took the apple from his pocket. "Want a bite?" he asked Mike.

"No thanks." Mike picked up a long toolbox, and they set off down the path. "Your brother?"

"Yup," Brian answered in spite of the apple in his mouth. "I'm her brother."

"Stepbrother," Mary corrected softly. "Mike, this is Brian."

"How'd you get off the trail?" Mike asked. "I work part-time for the Park Service. I thought they were all clearly marked."

"We were never on a trail," Mary explained. "Our back yard borders the woods, so we made our own paths."

"Do you cut down trees?" Brian asked Mike.

"Naw. Mostly I clear fallen limbs off paths, trim bushes along the edges. It's a good outdoor job for after school and weekends. So, where do you live?"

"Lockwood Lane. The only house past the nature preserve," Mary explained.

"Hey, you live in that big old Victorian job? When I was a kid—like you"—Mike pointed to Brian—"me and this friend, Neil—you know Neil," he said to Mary. "We used to think that house was haunted. We'd go out there on Halloween and creep around looking in the windows. Scared ourselves to death, seeing ghosts." He laughed.

50

"Oooh." Brian's eyes were wide. "You think there are ghosts in our house?"

"Naw." Mike cuffed Brian on the arm. "I was just a kid. It was all in our heads. Because it's old and sits out in the woods alone, it's a great place to make up stories about. In Boy Scout camp we used to sit around the fire at night telling stories. Your house was in a lot of them. Your place and the deserted mansion at the beach."

"Did you ever tell any stories about Riverview Station?" Mary asked.

Mike looked puzzled. "Riverview Station? Never heard of it."

"What's Riverview Station?" Brian asked.

"Just a place I—uh—read about somewhere." Mary tried to come up with an explanation. "In a history book, I think. There isn't an old station in the nature preserve?"

Mike shook his head. "Not that I know of."

"Be pretty funny to have a station out here." Brian giggled. "I want to hear the stories you told in camp—about ghosts."

Mike looked at Mary. "I remember one. You want to hear it?"

Mary nodded. She'd gotten that feeling she hated. Self-conscious, they called it. Acutely conscious of self. Hands and feet too big. Words sounded dumb in her mouth.

"Now, you understand this is not the atmosphere for a ghost story. We should be sitting around a fire in the dark, jumping at our shadows as they move in the fire-light. Can you picture it?" Mike asked Brian.

"Yeah!"

"Okay. Here goes: a long time ago a man lived in that big house with the gingerbread trim out on Studwell Point. Your house. There was nothing else for miles around—just the house and the woods and the animals that lived in them. I've heard some of them were were-wolves."

Mary remembered her first look at the house, and the strange way she had felt.

"This man used to walk through these very woods, lonesome as the hooting of the owl that would follow him in the early dawn. He was a silversmith, and he'd be taking his wares either to market in the town or to the railway depot—" Here Mike paused a moment. "Come to think of it, Mary, there was always a railroad station in the story. Funny you should mention one. Anyway, he used to go through the woods to get to it.

"One cold winter night—it was just before first light—snow was coming down. It was fine powder when he started out, but got heavier as he went along. He walked and walked, the snow swirling and whirling faster and faster, until this forest of his, these woods that he knew like the back of his hand, became like a foreign land where he was a stranger.

"He was carrying a heavy load of silver: a fine hand-made tea set. When day seemed to refuse to come, and the snow was heavy underfoot, he realized he was in serious trouble. He left his silver in the hollow of a large old boulder and tried to save himself.

"Like a mouse in a maze, he went round and round, sometimes close to his own house, which was shielded from him by the whiteness. The snow got deeper and deeper, and every step grew harder and harder as he sank down in it. Finally, he fell.

"When the storm was over and the search parties went out, they found him frozen twenty feet from his back yard."

"Is it true?" Brian was wide-eyed.

"I don't know." Mike lowered his voice. "But they say that on stormy nights his ghost can be heard crying and moaning in the woods as he looks for his lost silver."

"Boy!" Brian hopped around. "Maybe we can find it."

Mike clapped him on the shoulder. "It's just a story, kid."

"You're a good storyteller," Mary said.

"Thanks, Mary." He smiled at her. "I'd be happy to tell you another anytime."

Mary felt her face growing hot again, and she turned away. "We'd better hurry a little, Brian," she said.

The story came up again at supper that night. It had made an impression on Brian, and he relished telling it to his mother and stepfather. "So, see, we live in a haunted house," he concluded the tale.

"That's nonsense," his stepfather said. "Just childish superstition. You're too big to believe in ghosts, Brian."

"Not that big, Sir John." Brian grinned.

"I think it's *wonderful* for children to exercise their imaginations," Annie said. "Think how dull the world would be if we only believed in what we could see—or if we all saw everything the same way. There's nothing wrong with believing in ghosts. Why, Henry James, or was it William James? I always get them mixed up. Like those two sisters who work in the library. I never know if it's Wilma or Helen that's signing out my books—"

"What about William James?" Mary's father prompted.

"He *believed*"—Annie emphasized the word—"in ghosts, and look at him. He was a *renowned* thinker. A *profound* man."

"Have some more pasta, Mary." Her father held out his hand for her plate.

"I've had enough, thanks," Mary said.

"Annie went to a lot of trouble with this recipe."

"Pasta *fah-johl.* Pasta *fah-johl.*" Brian thought it was a funny word, and he laughed.

"Just a little more, Mary?"

"No, *thank you.*" Mary sat up straight and looked directly at her father.

"Leave her alone, John," Annie intervened. "She knows when she's had enough. You'd think she was anorexic, the way you nag the child. Now, Julia Hagge had legs like sticks. You would look at her and think if she fell down, they would shatter. Her mother tried everything. Finally they put her in New York Hospital. They have a unit for people with eating disorders. I should have that problem."

"Is it time for Weight Watchers again?" Brian asked.

"No. I'm still getting into my size fourteens." Annie laughed.

"Last time Ma lost eighty-five pounds. That's like losing a whole person," Brian said. "Somebody Mary's size."

Everyone laughed except for Mary. She didn't see what was so funny about being fat. "I weigh a lot more than eighty-five pounds," she said. "It's more like a hundred and ten."

"Perfect," Annie said. "A perfect weight for your height. At five foot five, you probably wear a size eight. I have wardrobes in three sizes." She made a face.

"I'm finished," Brian announced. "Can I watch TV?"

"Won't do you much good," John Barrone said. "The reception's lousy."

"Aren't we ever going to get it fixed?" Brian complained.

"Not until they run cable out here."

"It stinks. I'm missing all my programs."

"I brought home a videotape," his stepfather announced.

This news was greeted with cheers until Brian and Mary found out it was *Citizen Kane*. When Brian heard it was a classic, he moaned. Mary had hoped to slip off to her room right after supper, but dared not use homework as an excuse again. She had to sit through the movie, which seemed interminable.

When it was finally over, Brian had fallen asleep on the couch. He did not wake up when his stepfather carried him upstairs. Mary walked up behind him. "Good night," he whispered over his shoulder as she opened the door to her little stairway. "Sleep well, princess."

Once in her room, Mary hurried into her nightgown. Then she took the *Science Today* article from her desk. Since her daytime excursion into the woods had failed, she would try a nighttime excursion. This time she would go beyond flying.

Mary's stomach was fluttery as she read the instructions for dream spinning. They seemed simple enough. First she was to write down where she wanted to go.

Mary felt compelled to see that station again.

She tore paper from her notebook. "Riverview Station," she wrote. It did not seem to be enough. "Sometime in the past," she added.

She read the phrases over and over. "Riverview Station. Sometime in the past." When she felt they were engraved on her mind, she moved to the next part of the exercise.

The article told her to "keep repeating the phrase while you spin your dream body. Stretch out your arms and spin like a top."

She lay down on the bed and tried to picture her dream body. She felt uneasy, but a vision of her flight the night before returned, and the landscape below bathed in a strange beauty. In her mind she saw again the train station with the river flowing past and the dim light within.

Now she could picture her dream body. She could see

herself rising from the bed, standing in the middle of the floor. Though surrounded by darkness, she was clearly visible in her white nightgown. She watched as her body turned, slowly at first; then faster and faster it spun and pirouetted until she was one with the motion, whirling and spinning through space and time . . . and she was at the train station.

She was standing on the platform alone. It was dark and cold. She watched as the train on the track in front of her moved out of the station. Slowly it chugged to the river and, crossing it, sent out its mournful wail, which was like a tangible presence on the night air as it wound itself around Mary.

Mary shivered and backed away, seeking the protection of the wall. Her hand touched glass, and she turned to peer in the window. A dim globe hung from the ceiling. Below it, benches were empty. The station was deserted.

In the distance, the whistle of the train sounded again, throbbing through the darkness. Mary ran from it, around the back of the station, to the far side of the platform. Poles stood like sentinels, barren of the horses that would be hitched to them.

Then Mary heard a new sound: the soft clop of a horse's hooves on gravel. Through the darkness, twin beams of light could be seen floating in the air, moving toward Mary. Closer and closer they came. Mary could not move. Though she willed herself to float, to fly, to flee the spot, an invisible force, magnet-like, held her.

The lights turned into lanterns on either side of a horse-

drawn coach. It moved through the clearing, and Mary heard the jingle of harness bells. It came to a stop in front of her.

A figure swung down from the carriage. A man in a tall hat took a lantern from its holder. He held the light up to Mary. She looked into a handsome, smiling face. He put a hand under her chin as he peered at her. "Here she is, Julia," he said, "and shaking like a leaf. We must take her home and warm her up."

Chapter 6

~~~~~~

Mary sat up. The covers were on the floor, and she was shivering. Her teeth were chattering. She could not seem to get warm. The night air at the train station had chilled her to the bone. The cold dark night had done it, or the eerie whistle of the train cutting like icicles to her heart.

She reached down and pulled up the covers. This is my quilt, she said to herself. I am in my room. I have had a dream. That is all.

Was that all? His handsome face smiled at her, welcoming, just inches from her own. She shivered, this time with pleasure.

Who was he? How did he know her? A figment of her imagination? A phantom of her mind? Mary struggled to understand, to find an explanation. His hand under her chin, that smile illuminated by the light of the lantern.

She sat up in bed, forcing herself awake, and stared out the window in front of her. Nothing could have made the real Mary go out there alone into the blackness. But her dream self sought out the woods, the station, yes, even the train.

Her thoughts troubled her, and Mary threw back the covers and got out of bed. She welcomed the cold, solid floor beneath her bare feet and the scratchy feel of her flannel robe as she wrapped herself in it. She would go downstairs and have some milk. When she was little, her mother had always brought her warm milk if she couldn't sleep.

She put on her slippers and tiptoed down the stair, avoiding the creaky step. On the second floor she stopped and listened. There was no sound. She made her way to the first floor in the dark. When she turned on the lights in the kitchen, they hurt her eyes at first. They were bright and glaring and seemed to lack warmth.

Mary poured herself milk and sat down at the counter. An issue of *National Geographic* was lying there. She flipped through it, squinting at the pages, seeing nothing.

"Mary?"

She jumped, startled by her father's voice behind her. "Anything wrong?"

"No." She glanced at him over her shoulder, then quickly looked away. "Just couldn't sleep, that's all."

She heard him at the refrigerator, pouring milk. Then he pulled a stool up next to her.

"So what do you think, pal? How's it going?"

Oh, no, Mary thought. Here she was, feeling weird, and Daddy wanted to have a *talk*.

"Sam?" he prompted.

"It's okay."

"Is that a C or a B minus?"

"Sometimes I wish we'd never left Freedom." Mary blurted out words she had not meant to say.

"I hung in for four years after your mother died, Mary." Her father sounded sad, weary. "That town seemed to shrink after she was gone. Face it. It's a little hick town. Look at the schools. You weren't getting a top-notch education, while here——"

"Forget it, Daddy. This is a strange conversation to be having in the middle of the night."

"Of course. But we haven't had much chance to talk since the wedding . . ."

He went on, explaining, wanting Mary to give him the reassurance he needed.

"After your mother left us, you and I rattled around in that house like a couple of ghosts."

Those words sunk in. But it was *our* house, she wanted to say back to him. You and I were together.

"I wanted this to be a new start for both of us. I feel as if you're hanging back."

Mary shrugged. "I try."

"I know. I don't mean to lecture you. Just give this family your best shot. Okay?"

"Okay." Mary finished her milk and stood up. Her father reached out and took her hand.

"You're my sweetheart, Sam."

She squeezed his hand, suddenly tempted to tell him about her dream.

"Is there something else?"

A voice in her head sounded a warning. He wouldn't understand, and he wouldn't like it. He might forbid her to dream.

Mary shook her head. She picked up her glass and took it to the sink. "I'm going up now, Daddy."

"Sleep tight."

"You too."

"Sweet dreams." He smiled at her.

"Oh, yeah." The simple expression made her want to laugh. She picked up *National Geographic*. Maybe she could read herself to sleep.

The bed had to be entirely remade. She tucked in the bottom and sides and slipped in, feeling more secure.

Mary leafed through the magazine until she found an article about life in the hill towns of Italy. She tried to concentrate on the words, but soon her eyes grew heavy. She turned off the light and settled into her sleeping position, lying on her side. She seemed to have just gotten comfortable when the sound began.

At first she thought it was a foghorn, calling from the distant harbor. But then it sounded again.

She recognized the long, drawn-out wail of a train whistle.

Whoo-oo-oo-oo. Whoo-oo-oo-oo. Whoo-ooo-oooooo.
It rose higher and higher.

She sat up in bed, frightened.

It was almost a human howl.

She heard it again and scrambled out of bed, down the stairs, and through the door to the second floor.

There was a scream.

She turned to run to her father's room. Something hit her ankles, and she tripped, falling headlong on the floor. "Help!" she yelled.

"The ghost! The ghost! Mommy, help!" It was Brian hollering, and it scared her even more.

"Help!" she bellowed.

The hall light went on. Brian was sprawled across her legs. "What in the world?" Her father was standing over them.

"Mommy!" Brian jumped to his feet and ran past his stepfather to his mother. "I saw the ghost! I saw the ghost!" His voice rose to a shriek.

"Mommy's here, baby. Mommy's here."

Mary sat up, dazed. Annie was hugging Brian.

"The ghost was looking for the silver," Brian sobbed.

"There is no ghost, Brian. Get a hold of yourself," her father said.

"I tell you I saw him!"

"Well, it's Mary you tackled." He reached down and pulled Mary to her feet.

"I heard something," Mary said.

"You heard your brother having a nightmare."

"No. I heard a train whistle. It was eerie. It scared me."

"A train whistle? Is this whole family going nuts? Brian sees ghosts and you hear train whistles!"

"Now, take it easy, John," Annie pushed her hair back from her face. "The children had a scare. It's no use scolding them. They weren't trying to create a ruckus, for heaven's sake. Brian was sleepwalking and Mary had a bad dream. Why, honey," she said to Mary, "I take the prize for dreams. When I was eight months pregnant with Brian, I dreamed I was an elephant and had to stick my head out of the sun roof of the VW I drove then." She laughed and squeezed Brian. "Dreams are a sign of an imaginative person."

"I wasn't dreaming."

"Obviously, you were," her father said. "We're at least four miles from the station. I've never heard a train from here."

Mary shrugged her shoulders. "Well, I just did," she muttered.

"It seemed real," Annie soothed. "Dreams can be so vivid you'd swear they were true."

"Boy," Brian said. "I've never been so scared. When I woke up, I looked out my window. I just had the feeling that guy was out there walking around. It was real creepy. Then I come out of my room, and I see this big dark shape—"

"What guy did you think was out there?" Mary's father interrupted.

"The one Mike told us about," Brian said. He looked past his mother at his stepfather, his eyes wide. "Remember? He goes around moaning and looking for the silver he lost."

"That's nonsense!"

"Mike said a lot of people tell stories about this house being haunted." Brian stuck out his lip.

"And I don't want you to listen to any more of them, young man. This one has your imagination working overtime."

"It was just a story, Brian." Annie stroked his head.

"It's three in the morning. I suggest we all get to bed."

"I don't know if I can sleep." Brian looked up at his mother.

"Maybe you want to sleep on the chaise in our room. Just for tonight?" Annie suggested.

"No." Before Brian had a chance, his stepfather answered. "Brian's a big boy. Can't let your mother make a baby out of you. Right, son?" He patted Brian's shoulder.

"I guess not." Brian looked down at the floor.

"We'll leave our door open." John Barrone's tone was kind. "Then you can always call us if you get scared. Now, I'm tired, and we have to get up early. So, off to bed."

Mary slowly climbed the stairs to her room. No one had suggested she leave her door open.

She sat on the edge of her bed, her eyes getting used to the darkness. She did not want to go back to sleep. She was struggling to understand what was happening. Her father insisted there was no train whistle, while Annie blithered on about her silly dreams.

Mary knew she had heard it. The whistle had sounded a warning. It did not matter that no one else could hear it. There was an explanation for that. The train had pulled out of Riverview Station. It had left that station sometime in the past.

Mary walked over to the window and looked out at the back yard. The woods formed a solid, dark, impenetrable mass. The mystery lived in those woods, and like it or not, the nighttime Mary was drawn to them.

Chapter 7

The dream haunted Mary all week. Like a vignette, it played over and over. She could feel the cold at the train station. She could hear the lonesome call of the train. She could see the man's eyes in the light of the lantern and feel his touch, like a caress, on her face.

Nightly, she considered dreaming again. All she had to do was repeat the formula, and she would be at Riverview Station, sometime in the past. Perhaps she would get in the carriage. Perhaps she would meet Julia.

But still, she did not dream. She put it off from night to night, and daily, it seemed more and more fantastic. She had no proof, after all, and gradually she became convinced that it was just her mind playing tricks on her. She'd gotten carried away because of one article in a magazine.

Saturday morning, Mary put on warm clothes. She was determined to prove to herself that Riverview Station was a figment of her imagination. Mike said there was no train station, and he should know, but she would make sure.

When she got downstairs, she found her father and Annie in a tense conversation. "Brian should not be out there alone," Annie was saying.

"He's a boy. Boys like to explore."

"He's a diabetic. He could have an insulin reaction." Annie handed Mary a note. "Look at this."

Up early. Out treasure hunting.
Come on out, Mary-Mary.

Brian J. Delahaney.

"Honey." John Barrone waved an empty cereal bowl at Annie. "He ate breakfast. You fuss over him too much."

Mary handed the note back to her stepmother. "I'll go look for him." She could not help sighing at her own plans being spoiled.

"I'm going to call and cancel my appointment. I was supposed to show a house this morning, but I'm going with you." Annie reached for the phone.

"No. Don't do that," Mary said quickly. She could just see Annie crashing through the bushes, chattering away.

"That's absolutely unnecessary," John said. "Mary is very adept in the woods. The 4-H in Freedom had a

terrific nature program. She'll find Brian, though I doubt
if he's in any trouble."

"Are you sure?" Annie hesitated, her hand on the
receiver.

"He probably went the same way we did last weekend. I'll bring him right back."

That settled it. Annie loaded Mary's pockets with
food—packages of crackers and a chocolate bar. "If he's
sweating at all, give him this. Sugar is an immediate
antidote. It's like watering a drooping flower and watching it straighten up. It's amazing."

Annie was still calling instructions as Mary crossed the
back yard and entered the woods. The grass was wet
with morning dew. Chilly drops shook down on her hair
and clothes as she pushed branches aside.

When she came to the clearing where they had
rested, she saw that her bandanna was gone. She picked
up the path that led to the brook, half expecting to see
the deer. When none appeared, she started down to the
place where they had crossed the stream. Seeing a
splotch of color farther on, she stayed with the bank.
Her bandanna was tied to a birch tree. Mary smiled.
Brian had left her a clue. She untied the bandanna and
put it in her pocket.

Perhaps a hundred yards beyond, slate ledges rose in
front of her, making passage difficult. There was a path
of sorts to her right, and she veered off in that direction.
As she got deeper into the woods, she became confused
and worried. The path had opened into many possible
routes. She had no idea which Brian had taken.

A crow's hoarse squawk shattered the silence. It was joined by another, then another. She looked up and saw them, big, ugly, black vulture-like creatures. The sky was filled with them. In the distance, she could see them circling, and those overhead shrieked in their pursuit of the leaders. Carrion crows. The very words made her shiver.

Mary quickened her pace. The trees were smaller and gave way to a clearing where long grasses were spotted with blueberry bushes. Where the grass was still wet, it was trodden down in places. Animals could have been the cause, but she told herself Brian had come this way.

She called his name, and the sound of her voice in the largeness of the woods made her feel alone. There was no answer, save for the harsh cawing of the crows. It grew darker, and Mary realized that the sun had disappeared into a gray overcast sky. She wished she had not come by herself.

No trail presented itself. The crows were dropping down, out of her sight. They had found something. Frightened, Mary pushed on in their direction.

She came to an embankment and scrambled up. At the top her toe caught, and she tripped, sprawling on the ground. Trying not to cry, she pushed herself up on hands and knees. Something dug into her ankle. She felt around, and her hand encountered metal. She slid back into a sitting position to look further. Though grass had grown up around it, she had stumbled over an old train track. The wood had been reclaimed by nature, but the iron rods had endured.

Trains *had* run here.

Mary got up, and brushed herself off. She followed the tracks, conscious of her heart thudding in her chest. Through the trees, she made out the shape of a building ahead. She ran. The embankment leveled out, and she came into the open.

On her right was a dilapidated structure. The sagging, shingled building was surrounded by a platform that had settled into several levels. Part of the roof was missing, and the windows were broken.

Her breath caught in her throat, and she made a strangled sound. Time had broken down the building, but it looked like the train station in her dreams. She began to tremble.

A line of crows hunched along the overhang. On the platform beneath them, Brian slouched with his head cradled in his arms.

Mary ran up to him. He was dripping with sweat. She grabbed his shoulders. "Brian!"

He moaned.

Mary lifted his chin. His pupils were dilated and enormous. "Brian! It's me. It's Mary!"

He frowned as if bewildered.

"Brian!" Mary shouted, trying to get through to him. She pulled the candy bar out of her pocket and tore off the paper.

His head dropped down again when she released it. She tilted his head back and put a small piece of chocolate on his tongue. She was terrified he would choke, but she did not know what else to do.

"Swallow, Brian," she pleaded. "Let it melt on your tongue and swallow."

It seemed forever until she saw his Adam's apple move. "Good boy," she breathed softly. "Good boy."

She broke off a larger piece of the chocolate and put it in his mouth, unconsciously chewing and swallowing in sympathy. She took out a tissue and wiped his wet forehead. "That's it," she said as he swallowed.

"Mary?"

She wasn't sure he recognized her.

"I'm right here, Bri," she said, feeding him more candy. He chewed it slowly.

Mary continued to blot up the sweat on his face. She waved the Kleenex in front of him to cool him down.

"How are you doing?" she asked when the candy was nearly gone.

"Still weak," he answered.

Mary was really worried. She wondered if he would be able to walk back home. "Maybe I should go get my dad," she said.

"No. Please!" Brian pulled away from her supporting hand. "I'll be all right soon."

"Eat these, and we'll see." Mary fished a package of peanut butter and crackers out of her jacket and undid the cellophane. The food finally worked, and color came back into her stepbrother's face.

They sat quietly as Brian regained his strength. The woods around them were still, and Mary's relief over Brian's recovery was soon replaced by an uneasy feeling, as if someone were looking over her shoulder. She glanced around. No one. She was being ridiculous.

"Thank you for coming after me," Brian muttered.

"You led me to the station."

"Huh?"

"Nothing." It seemed impossible that she had seen this platform before, had stood here on a dark and cold night. It had been like a secret game, mulling over her dreams, imagining they were supernatural. Now, confronted by the reality of this railroad station, Mary was frightened. Though she had been searching for it, she had not really wanted to find it.

Perhaps it was only a weird coincidence. She jumped off the platform. The sudden move startled the crows. They took off in a flurry of beating wings and hacking calls to reassemble like black tumors on the branches of a nearby tree.

Mary shuddered. She turned from them and stared up at the peaked roof. There was no sign saying RIVERVIEW.

She clambered up the slight incline to the overgrown tracks and ran down to a riverbank, where they ended. There *was* a river, but no bridge spanned it.

She became aware of Brian panting behind her, and she put her arm in front of him, holding him back. "Careful. It's steep."

"What are you doing? What are you looking for?" Brian gasped.

"Nothing," Mary said. "Nothing. I—I just wanted to see the river."

"I don't believe you." He tugged on her sleeve. "You're all pale and scared-looking. You think he's around here, don't you?"

"Who? What are you talking about?" Mary looked at him, eyes wide.

"The old guy with the silver. Or"—he rolled his eyes, looking from side to side, and his voice became a whisper—"his ghost."

"Don't be silly!" Mary snapped, angry with herself for being afraid. "That's just a story."

"Mike said he was looking for a train station, and we found a train station," Brian insisted.

"And I'm going to look at it." Mary strode down the tracks. "I never heard anything so ridiculous—ghosts!"

Back on the platform, Mary walked over and looked in a window. A pane was broken. The rest of the glass was filthy, and the inside was covered with thick spiderwebs. She could not see the interior clearly.

She took a deep breath and went over to the center of the building, where a door hung by one hinge. She pulled it open, then rubbed her dirtied hands on her jeans. Brian followed her inside. The floor was rotten in places, and she felt her way carefully.

There were wooden benches like the ones in her dream. Their iron legs were rusted, and some had partially sunk through the wooden planks beneath them. Mary looked up. The lighting fixtures were gone and wires dangled from the ceiling.

To her left was a vertical double door, the top half standing open; the bottom half was topped by a small counter. They pushed it open and went inside. On the wall hung a round, wooden clock with a short pendulum. It was stopped at 2:05. Wooden cubbyholes lined the wall on one side of the door; ticket rolls unwound from large spools on the other side. Leaves and dirt had piled up in corners and along the baseboard, blown in through broken windows and the hole in the caved-in roof.

Mary tried to tear off a ticket. The end of the roll disintegrated in her hands. When she reached for another, the tickets would not separate. They were stuck together, probably from dampness.

"Hey, look at this!"

Mary turned to Brian, who was holding up a square wooden sign. Most of the letters were obscured by the dirt of years, but some were readable. *N, Y,* and *K* were visible near the bottom of the board.

Mary pulled the bandanna from her pocket and wiped away the grime.

"NEW," Brian read as the letters emerged. "NEW YORK/ 50 CENTS. Boy, that was cheap," he said.

Mary did not answer. She scrubbed furiously at the letters. SPRINGDALE/40 CENTS was right above New York. Names of three more places appeared as Mary worked her way up the sign.

One line was left. Mary hesitated.

"Come on," Brian urged. "Clean it off."

Mary reached toward the sign. She felt as if she were about to take an irrevocable step. Her hand jerked involuntarily as she wiped away the last layers of dirt. She stared at the words: STATION—RIVERVIEW.

Chapter 8

Now Mary would find out if she could trust Brian. Although she could not explain her reasons, even to herself, she had made him promise to keep the train station a secret. He had been grateful when she agreed not to mention his severe insulin reaction to his mother. So he would probably keep his word.

She tried to put the station out of her mind, but she could not. It was getting more and more difficult to pay attention in classes. She would start out listening to the teacher or reading an assignment, but somehow the dark building of her dream would steal into her consciousness. Sometimes it was like a double exposure. She would see the ruin of the present superimposed on the building of the past. Suddenly a bell would ring, and a whole class period would have gone by without her knowing it.

On Sunday afternoon she went to her room, determined to attack her homework. She got out her math book. She was so far behind that she could not follow the teacher when she put illustrated examples on the board. Now Mary would have to go back and work through several exercises by herself.

Mary opened her book and took out scratch paper. She read through the sample exercises that demonstrated how to find the value of x. The problems seemed simple enough, but when she tried to work one, she could not get the answer. It was hard to concentrate.

Voices from outside floated up to her slightly opened window: voices and laughter from a distance. The sound of rumbling wheels rolled across the air.

Mary crossed to a window. Brian and her father were pulling an old wagon across the front lawn. Annie had a basket full of pumpkins. As Mary watched, they piled them in the wagon. They were setting up a Halloween display.

Mary was tempted to go down, but she walked back to the desk. She would join them later after she finished her math. She stared at the pages of the book. The words would not register.

She had been fighting her desire to dream. Maybe that was a mistake. If she dreamed now, it would probably clear her mind so she could concentrate.

The article from *Science Today* was in the top drawer.

She reread the instructions: "Write down and commit to memory the person and place you want to visit."

She swallowed, wondering if it was wrong to dream in the daylight. She picked up the pencil, and on the paper where she had tried to find the meaning of x, she wrote, "The dark man and Julia. The past." There. It was done.

"If you have a question for the person, write it down. Picture yourself saying it to him or her."

That was easy. Why had they come to the train station? What was she to them?

"What am I to you?" she wrote.

She lay on the bed and closed her eyes. She pictured Riverview Station. She imagined the man smiling at her as she asked, "What am I to you?"

She pictured herself standing, arms outstretched. She tried to spin her body, but it would not move. She felt heavy and clunky. Then she realized why. She was picturing herself in sneakers.

She changed the Nikes to ballet slippers. She saw herself in a light blue dress instead of jeans.

Her body began to turn, slowly at first. Then it gained momentum. She could see the skirt flare out and her hair lift off her neck as she whirled and whirled. Her dream body was spinning like a top. She felt the motion.

"What am I to you? What am I to you?"

The question went round and round in her mind as her body went spinning through space.

Mary was in the garden, where dogwood trees had turned to copper. From the cottage she heard music once again—a piano, and this time, a woman's voice, light and delicate, raised in song. She looked in the window but saw only a reflection: a young woman, dressed in white, with full skirts that floated almost to the ground. The girl had ash-blond sausage curls cascading over her shoulders. She looked light as air.

As Mary lifted her hand to her own hair, so did the image in the glass. Mary felt the wide straw brim of a hat and saw her double look at her in wonder.

"Who am I?" Mary formed the soundless words.

Something drew her eyes upward to the tower room, her room. He was standing there by the open window, listening to the music. He lifted his hand, acknowledging her, and smiled. He was very handsome, tall and elegant.

The song finished and the playing stopped. The cottage door opened, and a woman came out. Her dark hair, parted in the middle, framed violet eyes. She came directly to Mary and kissed her on the cheek. Then she walked past her and looked up at the tower. Her green-and-white-checked dress had a bustle in back. Her hair was beautifully coiled.

The man touched his fingers to his lips and blew her a kiss. She laughed.

"Get to work, Charles," she called.

"I'd rather listen to you, Julia," he replied.

"Then why did I move my piano to the summerhouse? I did not want to disturb my talented husband."

"You always disturb me, my darling," he answered.

"You are a scandal, sir." Julia laughed. "You will shock our darling little guest. Come, dear." Julia turned to Mary and took her hand.

They walked down a brick path, bordered by flowers. Julia leaned over and picked a large yellow chrysanthemum. She handed it to Mary. Mary held it up to her nose. There was no odor. The blossom floated out of her hand onto the grass.

The lawn was mowed and carefully edged. Mary remembered her scraggly, overgrown back yard and realized she was dreaming.

An opening in the stone wall led to a wide, sunny path through the woods. "This is a shortcut to the train station," Julia said.

The train station. They were going to the train station.

"We brought you home in the carriage. It is the long way round."

They were in a meadow. Golden grasses reached to their knees, moving in the sunlight as a breeze stirred them. Blue-green bushes with deep blue berries were sprinkled across the field.

"Beautiful!" Mary said softly. "Like a painting."

"Juniper bushes," Julia said.

Julia and Mary glided across the field. "Mind the stile," Julia warned.

Soon they were on a dirt road. "Now we're back on Ketchum Wood Road, and the shortcut saved us a mile. We bought the house so Charles can walk from the station if he is late returning from New York."

Mary wanted to say something, but only the question spun about in her mind. It was too crude to ask. She was staying with Charles and Julia. That much was clear. But who was she?

80

A horse and buggy approached. As they went by, they raised dust. Mary was surprised at how thick it was. It got in her eyes, and she could not see. It swirled around and around, circles of dizzying dust that caught her up and twisted her into motion. She turned and turned on the points of her toes like a ballet dancer.

"What am I to you? What am I to you?"

Chapter 9

Mary drifted through the week, silent and remote. She wandered in the back yard, arranging it again in her mind as she had seen it in her dreams. She started to go in the summerhouse where Julia used to play the piano, but was stopped by her father. It looked unsound, he told her. He would have a builder look at it and see if it was worth restoring.

Even in school, Mary could not shake her mood. "You always disturb me, my darling," she heard Charles call over the drone of her computer teacher. She looked in surprise at her screen. The words were there. She moved the cursor back, erasing them, but she could not erase them from her mind.

In art class, while others sketched a bowl full of fruit or an arrangement of vegetables, her apple turned into the bustle of Julia's dress; then she sketched in the rest of her outfit. At the sound of her teacher's footsteps she hastily tore the page off her sketch pad.

"Let's see," the teacher said.

"It was terrible." Mary scrunched up the drawing. "I'll try another."

On Wednesday in English, the class read silently while Ms. Martinez had individual conferences. Mary looked at the section of *The Odyssey* where Odysseus' crew met up with the lotus eaters. When the men ate the lotus flower, they lost their desire to return home. They were under a spell. She was staring at the questions at the end of the section when she became conscious that someone was standing by her desk.

She looked up. Mike Bell flashed that crinkly grin. "Finding your way around the Myanous?"

Mary nodded. More than you know, she thought.

"I picked up a map for you. It has all the trails marked." He handed her a thick, folded paper.

"That was really nice of you," Mary said.

" 'Sall right. Maybe we'll bump into each other out there again sometime."

"Mike, I would appreciate it if you could get from the back of the room to my desk without a stop," Ms. Martinez chided.

"Sorry," he apologized. "Later," he said to Mary.

Mary pushed her book to the top of her desk and unfolded the map in front of her. It was easy to locate the river, but there was no mark to indicate the train station. She studied the map. If her calculations were correct, the nearest marked trail was some distance from the site. It was odd that a landmark like that had been allowed to be swallowed up by time and the woods.

"Mary." Ms. Martinez interrupted her thoughts. She hastily folded the map and went up to the desk.

"How is your project coming? Have you heard from the university?"

Mary shook her head.

"Then you'd better take another tack. Time's going by. I mentioned your project to Mrs. Bermingham in the Media Center. She'll see what she can find on authors who have been influenced by dreams." Ms. Martinez looked at her watch. "There's about fifteen minutes left in the period. Go on up and talk to her."

Mary found Mrs. Bermingham in the English section of the library. She was a small lady with short white curly hair and bright blue eyes. She always seemed to be smiling. "Hello, Mary," she said. Mary was surprised that in such a big school the librarian remembered her name.

"Ms. Martinez told me to come and see you," Mary said.

"And you want to research authors who have been influenced by dreams?"

"No. That's what Ms. Martinez wants me to do."

Mrs. Bermingham laughed. "That's an honest answer. And what is it Mary would like to do?"

"I don't know. I just can't see doing some boring old report."

"Well, what are your interests? We should be able to find some subject that won't be boring."

"I'm interested in . . ." She couldn't say a couple who lived in the past and the girl who lived with them. "Uh . . . the history of this town." The idea had come to her suddenly. She could find out about the past while she did her project.

"That doesn't sound like a subject for English—social studies maybe." Mrs. Bermingham bit her lip. "Unless . . . you investigate authors who have lived here. At the moment we have several famous writers in Sound Port. I'm sure we've had many in the past. What do you think?"

Mary shrugged. "Maybe."

Mrs. Bermingham was enthusiastic. "You could find writers representative of several eras or concentrate on one period. Or you could find writers who used the town in their writing. This should be a wonderful project!"

"Do you have any books on Sound Port's history?"

"Very few, but I'll tell you where to go. The Sound Port Historical Society. Ever been there?"

"No."

"It's in the Preble-Dickey House; oldest house in town. Worth a visit on its own. Here are directions." The librarian drew a map on a piece of paper. "Let me know how your project develops."

After school, Mary called her father in his landscape office and arranged for a ride home at five o'clock.

It was over a mile to the Preble-Dickey House. Mary had just started up the last long hill when a car pulled over to the curb. Noisy teenagers seemed to be spilling out of it. "Want a ride, Mary Barrone?" She looked up to see Mike Bell hanging out a window. There didn't seem to be room to squeeze in another person.

"No thanks," she said softly.

"These opportunities don't come along every day." He raised his eyebrows, mock serious. Then he waved, and the car drove off.

Mary watched it go up the hill and out of sight. She wished she could have said okay, but she just couldn't. She might have had to sit on Mike's lap, and that would have embarrassed her to death. She should have made a joke at least. "Sure, Mary," she said to herself sarcastically, "you're really good at jokes."

This was no time to get down on herself. She had her project to think about. The Historical Society was the perfect place to find out about the past. There might even be a way to find out about Charles and Julia. The thought excited her, and she hurried up the hill.

At the top there was a sign for the Preble-Dickey House. An arrow pointed to a long driveway. Mary turned left and walked down to a low, rambling, shingled building that looked out over Long Island Sound. A small card on the front door read KNOCK AND ENTER, which Mary did.

There was no one in the entrance hall. "Hello?" Mary called.

"In here." The answer came from a room off to the left. Inside what looked like an old-fashioned study, a heavy, middle-aged woman was sitting at a desk. She greeted Mary with a smile and asked her if she would like a tour of the house.

"That sounds nice," Mary said, "but I only have an hour or so, and I'd like to get some background on the history of Sound Port."

"You're in luck," the lady said. "Hartley Gray is the volunteer today. He knows more about this town than any other living person. And he loves to talk about it!"

Hartley Gray was shelving books in the library. He was an older man with thinning gray-brown hair, wire-rimmed spectacles, and a round face that had few wrinkles.

"I brought you this young lady who is interested in doing some research on Sound Port."

"Glad to have you," Mr. Gray said. "Since I've retired, local history has been my hobby. Some would say my obsession."

"I leave you in good hands." The lady who had brought her in backed toward the door.

"Thanks, Lydia." Mr. Gray waved to her. "What is your name?" he asked, turning to Mary.

"Mary Barrone."

"What are you looking for, Mary? What aspect of Sound Port's history do you want to examine?"

Mary hesitated, torn between duty and desire—her report and her dreams.

Local authors could wait. "Railroad stations," she said.

"That's unusual," Hartley Gray answered. "I don't know why I say that, though. Railroads have been important here since they started. First steam passenger train was operated by the New York and New Haven Railroad. Began running on Christmas Day of 1848."

So her railroad station existed sometime after that, Mary thought.

"Would you have a book on railroad stations in Sound Port?" Mary asked.

"Not one that deals just with railroads. We did a book for the bicentennial. It has pictures of all aspects of life in Sound Port since 1776." He walked over to a shelf and pulled out a large book. "There'll be some information in here."

At one end of the room was a polished oval table and two straight-backed chairs. "Come and sit down," Mr. Gray said, placing the book on the table. "We'll have a look." He opened the cover and began leafing through the pages. He stopped at a picture of a huge, rambling house with a porch on all sides. "That was a summer 'cottage.' Pretty swell, huh?"

"Uh-huh," Mary said.

He turned the page and pointed to a picture of a little house on the water. A dock stretched almost to the front door. "This, on the other hand, was the home of a year-round resident. Probably a lobsterman."

Mary tried to look interested. She wished he would turn the pages faster. She tapped her foot impatiently.

"Look at this. It's a picture of Rocky Point Island. There's a great story about this place. You see these rocks breaking the surface?" He pointed to dark spots in the water. "Reefs and ledges surround the island, except for a narrow channel. A wicked old feller lived there in the eighteenth century. On stormy nights, he would put a lantern around his horse's neck and take him down to the shore. Ships looking for safe harbor in the storm would steer for the light. They'd shipwreck on the rocks."

They'd never find her station at this rate, Mary thought. All he wanted to do was tell stories.

"When daylight came and the storm had passed, Kingsley—that was his name—would row out and steal the cargo. He'd kill any survivors and bury 'em on the island." Mr. Gray looked at her, waiting for a reaction.

"What an awful man," Mary said.

She must have sounded uninterested, Mary realized, because Mr. Gray apologized.

"I helped put this book together," he said. "Just about every picture reminds me of some bit of history. But I don't have to tell you all of it in one day. 'Fraid I get carried away. But if you want to do research on railroads, I'd better get back on the track," he joked.

"Aha." He pointed to a picture. "There's Sound Port Station, circa 1870."

Mary felt her shoulders sag. It was not the station in the woods. "Was this the only one in town?" she asked.

"Oh, no. There were two others. One in Old Sound Port and another in what is now Congregation. Used to be called Riverview."

"Riverview?" Mary sat forward. "Did you say Riverview?"

He looked at her quizzically. "That one interest you particularly?"

"Yeah. Well. I—like the name, I guess." Mary shrugged, trying to look nonchalant.

"Pictures here somewhere." He turned more pages. "Riverview was abandoned years ago. Thirties, probably. More year-round people by then, and new lines were built to service areas of greatest density. Riverview was torn down."

"Oh, no," Mary said.

"Well, yes, it was. In the depression. FDR started the WPA. Out here they worked on the railroad, shifting it about. There!" He pointed, satisfied. "I knew there was a picture."

And there it was. The sign was clear above the station. Women in long dresses sat on the platform where she had found Brian.

Mary could feel her heart beating, making a loud noise in her ears. The photograph of the station looked exactly as it had in her dreams. She leaned down, peering at it eagerly. Perhaps Julia was one of the women on the platform!

"You can make a copy of this picture if you want."

Mary sat back abruptly. She must not act too eager. "Thank you," she said.

"What's this research for, by the way?" Mr. Gray asked.

"An English report," Mary answered, choosing her words carefully. "Of course, it will have to include more than train stations. I'd like to look at other things, too— like photographs of people. I want to study the way they lived."

90 ∽

"Sounds like you're covering a great deal for one report."

"I'm not exactly sure how I'm going to put it together yet. But I'm *so* interested in the town and its history, I'm sure I'll find a way to use the material."

"There were people who lived in this town who'd make great characters in a short story, Mary. They might fit into your English paper. Take John Honey. Inappropriate name if I ever heard one. Lived here in the early days of the century. John Honey was a bum. He was always in trouble—drunkenness, petty thefts; that kind of thing."

Mary wished she hadn't gotten Mr. Gray started on another story. She licked her lips.

"John Honey would take up winter residence in the homes of summer people. He was in and out of jail." Mr. Gray shook his head and smiled, obviously enjoying himself. "The townspeople got tired of paying for his room and board in the hoosegow. Even then, there were no free lunches in Sound Port."

Mary forced a smile.

"Well, they exiled him to a little island in the Sound. Put him out there with bare necessities. John Honey lived there twenty years in the heat and cold. He got by on shellfish, lobsters, and birds."

Mary made a face.

"Not too appetizing, is it? Some of the fishermen would take pity on him and drop supplies now and again. Then, one winter, smoke stopped coming out of his shack. After a week, someone checked. Found poor

John Honey frozen to death." He paused, waiting for a reaction.

"That's terrible," Mary said.

"Think you could use it? Got all the elements. Man against man. Man against nature."

"Not really. But you have given me an idea," Mary said. "I live in an old house that there are stories about. Maybe I could write up one of them." She told him Mike Bell's story about the silversmith.

"I've heard a version of that one." Hartley Gray laughed. "The way it was told to me, the silversmith was out looking for his wife, who had run off with another man. So you're living out on Studwell Point?"

Mary nodded.

"That's a great old house. Guess your folks have their work cut out for them, fixing it up."

"Yes," Mary agreed, thrilled at the direction the conversation had taken. "Do you know anything about the history of the house?"

"Well, sure. Betty James, the lady you bought it from, was in my high school class. I'm going back some fifty years. Prettiest girl in school. But I hear, after her husband died, she got a little odd. Kept something like twenty cats. Became a recluse. Let the house decay."

"I meant earlier. Like, did a silversmith really live there?"

"Probably some truth to it. I can't say for sure, but I could nose around and find out."

"Would there be a way to trace all previous owners?" Mary asked. "I just feel there might be a story, and it would be fun to find out about my house at the same time." She was breathing fast. "I'd give anything to see some pictures of our place and the people who lived in it."

"All property transactions are a matter of record," Mr. Gray said. "Your dad must have had a title search done. His lawyer'd have a copy. Far as pictures, you might find something in this book. I don't rightly remember." He took a card from the back, inside cover. "Sign this, and you can borrow it. Of course, we have masses of photos that didn't get in it. I'll see what I can find."

Mary thanked him and promised to come back the next week. He was such a nice man, even if he did talk a lot. He would help her find out about Charles and Julia, and then she would write her story about them. Maybe she would even be in it.

Chapter 10

Mary's father had been waiting for her at his office. When they arrived home, they found Annie and Brian stripping wallpaper in the front hall. It was a mess.

"There must be sixteen layers!" Annie exclaimed. "I think I've hit plaster, and another color appears. Look at this." She pointed to a square area on the wall where she had removed the paper so that a small strip of each layer remained. "I could put a frame around this and call it art. Don't you think so?"

"Sure," John agreed. "You could call it 'Layers of Life at Studwell Point.'"

Mary looked more closely at the exposed strips of wallpaper. "Is this the original paper?" she asked, running her finger over a gold-and-maroon strip.

"Heavens, no," Annie said. "I may be down to the

1920s, but I won't hit the last century for days. I could just rip through it, but I don't want to miss any of the layers. They all tell stories. This top one is yellow and faded and dull—like the life that poor old woman lived who sold us the house. It was probably pretty when it was new, but age and neglect covered its beauty."

"You have some imagination." John beamed at her. "Nothing bores you—not even stripping wallpaper."

"Just look," Annie said. "The next layer down is a formal stripe. Her husband was still alive, and they were middle-aged and prosperous. They entertained a lot."

Annie continued telling her silly, made-up stories, which obviously tickled John. Mary didn't understand why.

"This is fun, Mary." Brian tore back a long piece of paper. "It's like peeling off your skin when you get a sunburn."

"That's disgusting!" Mary said, turning away.

"Hello?" There was the sound of footsteps bounding up the outside stairs. Mike Bell stuck his head in the front door, his hand resting against the side that was closed.

"Hi, Mike!" Brian stopped his work on the wallpaper and ran over to the door, smiling happily.

"Hi, kid." Mike ruffled his hair and cuffed him on the shoulder. "Hi, Mary. Am I busting in at a bad time?"

"No," Mary mumbled. She was shocked to see him standing in her doorway, yet she was acutely aware of his physical presence. It was as if an electromagnetic field were emanating from him.

Mike looked at Annie and her father, then at Mary, waiting to be introduced.

Brian broke the silence. "This is the guy who told us about the ghost. Tell Sir John, Mike. He doesn't believe the house is haunted."

"Hey, neither do I. I told you that was just a story." Mike held his hand out to her father. "I'm Mike Bell."

"This is my father, Mr. Barrone," Mary said hastily. "And this is—uh—Brian's mother—" That sounded ridiculous, and she tried again. "This is Mrs. Barrone."

"Annie Barrone," her stepmother said. "So you're the culprit who had us all awake at three in the morning— Brian seeing ghosts looking for silver; Mary hearing—"

"Ann—nie!" Mary could have died with embarrassment.

"Oh, well." Annie changed her tack. "No harm done. I can't say we didn't lose sleep over your story, however." It was clear from her tone that she was teasing.

"Sorry, Mrs. Barrone," Mike responded with a grin. "I'll be real careful what I tell Brian from now on."

"What are you doing here, Mike?" Brian asked. "You working at the nature preserve?"

"Not today, but I work all day Saturday. I don't have a lot to do, so I thought you guys might like it if I cleared a path from your back yard, and hooked you up with a trail. I won't be able to finish it this weekend, but I could make a start."

"Sounds like an excellent idea." John Barrone nodded. "Very nice of you."

"That would be *sen*-sational," Annie declared. "I can't fight my way through that jungle. I feel like a bushwoman thwacking through the brush. It would be *great!*"

Mike looked at Mary. She couldn't compete with her stepmother's enthusiasm, so she said nothing.

"Think you'll be taking a hike this weekend?" Mike asked.

Mary shrugged. "Maybe."

"I will," Brian offered.

"I'll start around eight on Saturday," Mike said, still looking at Mary. "I thought we could walk the area together, sort of plot out the course."

"Mary?" her father prompted.

"Yes. Okay." She hadn't meant to sound so irritable.

"Good," Mike said. "See you in English. And see you Saturday."

"See you," Brian agreed enthusiastically.

"Mary, he is *ad-or-able!*" Annie said, once Mike had left. "*You* certainly are a closed-mouth one. I had no idea this fellow you were meeting in the woods was so good-looking."

"Seems like a nice young man," her father said.

"Isn't it cute? The way he's building a new trail so he can see Mary? Talk about beating a path to your door." Annie giggled.

"Can't say I blame him." Her father smiled at her.

Mary didn't know why Mike Bell had chosen to be nice to her. She had seen some of the cheerleaders falling all over him, so he couldn't like her. It made Mary feel small, somehow, to have Annie and her father assume he did. She felt as if she were shrinking inside.

"You are just so dumb sometimes!" she said, the tears coming to her eyes.

"Honey!" John Barrone reached over, but Mary ducked away, evading his touch, and ran from the room.

"Dumb! Dumb! Dumb!" she repeated, running up the two flights of stairs. She slammed the door to her room, shutting out their voices calling her.

She picked up the hand mirror on her dresser and stared at her reflection. What could Mike see in the face that looked out of that glass? Eyes that changed from green to blue depending on what she wore. A full lower lip that was trembling now. Her skin was clear and soft, but so what? Curly hair—but not a true blond, kind of a light brown. There was no way she could compete with some of the girls he knew in school—girls who would be homecoming princesses.

She put the mirror down and covered her face with her hands.

"Mary?" Annie said softly.

"Just leave me alone, please." Mary sniffled.

There was a pause, and the door closed. Annie's footsteps resounded on the uncarpeted stairs.

Mary had refrained from dreaming on school days. But one time wouldn't matter, she told herself. She had been wanting to go back to Riverview since last Sunday, to make contact again with the beautiful woman and the handsome, laughing man who had lived here in her own house. Charles and Julia. She said the names aloud, then took a sheet of paper from her desk drawer. Maybe she could slip back for just a few minutes, just long enough to see the house.

"My house in Riverview," she wrote.

She lay down on the bed, pulling the quilt up under her chin. Then she closed her eyes and pictured her dream body rising from the bed and walking to the middle of the room. In her mind's eye, the dream body was luminous. She pictured herself spinning. "My house in Riverview," she repeated as she twirled. Again and again, faster and faster, she spun. "My house in Riverview—my house in Riverview—my house in Riverview—my house in Riverview . . ."

"Turn round again, dear." Mary's elbow was given a gentle push, and she swung about. "I think that outfit will do." Julia regarded her intently. "It's the tiniest bit provincial, but you look very sweet."

Mary looked down. She was wearing a blue dress made of heavy cotton with a gathered skirt, ruffled at the ankles. It was plain compared to Julia's shiny maroon silk, which was gathered across the front and formed a small bustle in the back.

"I shall dress you in green to accent those lovely eyes and to set off the blond lights in your hair," Julia said. "You will be the belle of Riverview."

The bedroom where they were standing was like a picture from a magazine. At one end a curtained bed filled an alcove. A satin chaise longue looked inviting under a window where heavy velvet drapes hung. There were several paintings on the walls. Mary recognized an oil of their house. "That's really good," she said.

"Thank you, dear child." Julia beamed. "I'm just a dabbler when it comes to painting, but I'm pleased you admire my efforts."

"Are the ladies ready?" Charles entered, carrying a top hat, a white silk scarf at his neck.

"I just have to wrap a present, Charles," Julia replied.

"What are we giving the little fellow?" Charles asked.

"I've bought him his first sailor suit, though it won't fit him for months, and I knit him a carriage robe. You've seen that as I worked on it, I think, darling. Then there's a silver rattle. Every child should have a Tiffany rattle."

"I thought you said a present. Sounds like you've done rather a lot for a second cousin, once removed."

"I said I have to wrap a present. I didn't say I had only one." She turned her head away. "I enjoy getting baby things."

"Well, that's all right, then." Charles put his hands on his wife's shoulders and lightly kissed the top of her head. He looked over at Mary. "Would you do me a favor, my dear? I've left a box on my desk that I meant to take along, a little gift for the papa. Would you be good enough to fetch it for me?"

Mary must have looked confused, for Charles went on. "In the tower. That's where I work."

As Mary left the room, she saw Charles put his arms around Julia and murmur something to her.

Mary walked down the hall. The door to the third floor

100 ✑

was open. As she walked up, the third stair creaked, and she jumped, jolted into awareness of her real life.

The room was very different from the one she slept in. The windows were wavy glass, through which a dying sunset suffused the place with a red glow. She looked out the front window at a gravel drive, lined with thin, gray saplings. It hardly seemed possible they would become large, thick, spreading oak trees. She drifted over to the back and admired flower beds in matching circles, brick paths that formed a pattern, the summerhouse comple- mented by the grape arbor. The back yard was trans- formed into a garden of Eden.

Inside, the room had a definite masculine air. The walls were deep green with an ivory border. A small oriental rug was on the highly polished floor in front of a large oak desk. A partially finished page lay next to a typewriter that had funny, individual round keys, and a printing wheel. Perhaps the male aroma came from the pipe in the ashtray. Next to it was a small wooden box of cigars—what Mary had been sent to get.

As she reached for it, she looked down. Her arms and dress were bathed in red. Suddenly spooked, Mary snatched the box and hurried from the room.

"Chin up, darling," she heard Charles say as she came back.

Julia's reply was inaudible, but she pulled away from him and turned her attention to a small blue box on the bed. The paper she used for wrapping was patterned with ribbons and cherubs.

It was growing dark quickly, and Charles lit gas lamps

on the wall in the hallway. "I hope this won't be too tedious for you," he said to Mary on the way downstairs. "A lot of grownups fawning over a little, squalling creature. There will be more exciting events during your visit."

"There will be plenty of parties and balls to attend if you like," Julia said.

"Of course she would like. And so will we. I expect your beautiful young niece will keep us lively, Julia dear."

Niece!

In the downstairs hall, an older woman in a black uniform and white apron hurried up to Julia. She was carrying a black cape.

"I won't need that, Maude," Julia said. "It's very mild for November."

"It's freshened out there, missus. You'll catch your death. Now, be a good girl and put this on." Maude started to put the cape over Julia's shoulders, but she shrugged it off impatiently.

"I think you should," Charles said.

"Will you two stop fussing over me, please?" Julia went to the hall closet. "I'm not wearing that heavy thing." She held up a fringed shawl. "This will do nicely."

Outside, the wind was blowing, and Charles hurried them into the waiting carriage. He pulled a blanket from under the seat. He sat down between Julia and Mary, spreading the blanket over their laps, then put an arm around each of them.

"We're going to the Fergusons', Joseph," he told the driver.

"Very good, sir."

Wheels crunched on the gravel; the wind shook the sides of the carriage.

"You see it is cold when the sun goes down," Charles said, gripping them closer.

The carriage bounced along, the wheels creaked and turned, and the wind whistled. Their niece! Mary let her head rest against her handsome uncle's shoulder.

Chapter 11

∞∞∞∞∞∞∞∞∞∞∞∞∞∞∞∞∞∞∞∞∞

Outside, it was dark, and the moaning wind seemed to encircle and surround Mary's tower. It rattled the windows and seeped in the cracks, cold with the warning of winter.

"Charles!" Mary called aloud.

The sound of her own voice startled and half woke her. She looked down in surprise at her clothes—the sweatshirt and blue jeans seemed to belong to someone else.

Mary sat on the edge of her bed, then reached over and, fumbling, turned on the lamp. The light hurt her eyes.

There was a rapping. The downstairs door opened, and Brian's singsong intruded up the stairs. "Mary-Mary!"

"Go away!"

"Supper's ready. They sent me to tell you."

What was he talking about?

"You coming?"

"Just leave me alone. Okay?"

"Whatsa matter? You sick?"

Mary didn't answer. It was quiet for a moment; then she heard the door close and Brian hopping down the stairs to the first floor.

She was completely disoriented. Brian had said supper was ready, but it felt like the middle of the night. She had been asleep, so it should be morning.

She looked at the clock on the table by her bed: 7:30.

The wind sent the branches of the tall evergreen screeching and dragging over the roof, and Mary shivered. The windows rattled in their tracks.

"Mary!" Her father had come up the stairs and stood in the doorway. "What's going on here? What's this about not eating dinner?"

"I'm not hungry."

"If you're mad at us for teasing you about that young man . . ."

Then Mary remembered what had happened. That afternoon she had fallen asleep and dreamed her way back to Riverview.

"I'm sorry," her father said. "I really didn't know it would bother you. I guess we were insensitive. Annie says we were."

"Just drop it. Okay?"

"Well, then, come on down and have something to eat."

Mary sighed. She really wanted to go back to sleep, but she couldn't tell him that. And the wind might keep her awake. Then she'd be here alone—awake and alone.

"Mary?"

She got up slowly. "I'll just wash up."

"And comb your hair before you come to the table. Listen to that wind. Sounds a lot louder up here than downstairs. Makes me cold just to listen to it."

He started down the steps, but turned back. "Does it ever bother you? I hadn't realized what an eerie sound it makes, whistling around all these corners."

"No," Mary lied. She didn't want her father to get any ideas about moving her out of this room. This room belonged to her and to Charles.

"All right, then. Hurry it up a bit." He ran lightly down the stairs.

In the bathroom, Mary splashed cold water on her face. The bare yellow bulb over the mirror made her look pallid, like a washed-out version of the girl she had seen reflected in the window. She pulled a comb through her hair, then tried winding a lock around her finger to make a sausage curl. It recoiled, springing back to its own wave. Evidently it was only in dreams that she could be beautiful.

Mary was quiet through dinner, but no one seemed to notice. Annie filled any silence. She always had stories to tell about her real estate customers, or the plumber, or the painter. Everything was high drama or low comedy to Annie.

106

After dinner, Mary brought down the Sound Port Bicentennial book that Mr. Gray had lent her. It had a special meaning for her, and she pored over the pages, hoping to find a picture of Charles or Julia. During that week, the book became her substitute for dreaming, a way to resist the urge that overtook her daily.

She looked at graduation classes and skating parties, at town meetings and picnics. Grainy and indistinct, the photographs evoked a romantic past: the town blanketed in snow, young girls in long dresses, unpaved roads crossing a rural landscape.

On Friday evening she was studying again the picture of Riverview Station: the women in hats and bustles, sitting on the edge of the platform; the men, behind them, leaning against the building.

"Mary!"

"Huh?" Mary looked up at Annie, who was standing beside her.

"I've been trying to get your attention for five minutes. What is so fascinating?"

Mary felt like covering the page as Annie peered at it, nearsightedly. "Just something for English class."

"You're as absorbed as if you were reading a best seller. You are *wonderful*. Why, look at these old pictures. Don't you just love to see the clothes people used to wear? When people look back at pictures of our times, I suppose everyone will be in jeans. That's a depressing thought. I wonder what it says about us?"

Mary closed the book, but held her finger in the page.

"I didn't mean to interrupt," Annie said. "I just suggested to Brian that I pack you a picnic lunch tomorrow when you go out making trails."

"A picnic in November?" Mary asked.

"The temperature is going to be in the sixties," her father said. "Indian summer."

"Where did that expression ever come from?" Annie asked. "What makes a warm spell out of season an Indian summer? Why not an Eskimo . . ."

Mary opened her book again, but Annie chattered on, distracting her. Brian ran out of the room and came back with the map Mike had given Mary.

"Let's see that," her father said.

"Our house is right here." Brian pointed. "I figured it out and marked it with an *X*."

Mary tried harder to immerse herself in the past. If she concentrated, she could almost recapture her walk with Julia—the wide path, the meadow with the old-fashioned stile, the feel of the gravel road under her feet.

"Mary, there is a marked trail approximately three-quarters of a mile back from our property line. Come and take a look." Her father held out the map. "That's probably the one your friend will aim for."

Mary sighed. She put down her book and walked slowly over to his chair. He traced a line with his finger from the *X* to a green route. "It will be quite a project. Good one, though. Out of doors. Fresh air. I have some tools you can use. Brian, I have the perfect small saw for you."

"Hey, thanks, Sir John."

Mary forced a yawn, which prompted a real one. "Guess I'll go to bed."

John Barrone looked at his watch. "It is nearly eleven. Time for you, too, Brian."

"Good night." Mary kissed her father on the forehead. He took her arm, pulled her close, and kissed her on the cheek.

"Night, kiddo."

Mary straightened up. Annie was looking at her. "Good night." Mary lifted her hand slightly in Annie's direction. Annie blinked and swallowed. Mary knew she had disappointed her again.

As Mary left the room, she heard Annie say quietly, "Give me a kiss, Briny," and heard her father making an excuse for her. "Teenagers are awfully stingy with their kisses," he said.

Mary ran upstairs to her room. She undressed and put out the light. There was no moon, but there were stars in the dark sky.

She pulled back the covers and climbed into bed; closing her eyes and picturing the room as it used to be when it belonged to Charles. He must have looked out these windows and seen these stars. He might be doing that very thing even now, in another time. Or was his presence still in this room? And did it call to her over the years?

Like a patient under anesthesia, Mary floated in a twilight state. It was the morning sun that woke her, turning her room to pink. Out her windows to the east, the sky was streaked with reds and yellows. She had slept. It was a new day.

She turned over and closed her eyes again. "Charles and Julia in the late 1800s," she said. "Charles and Julia in our house in the late 1800s. Charles and Julia and me in our house in the late 1800s."

"Well, there you are, little sleepyhead." Julia gestured to a chair between Charles and her at the dining room table. "I thought you were going to miss breakfast."

"Doesn't Uncle Charles get a kiss?" He smiled and leaned toward Mary.

Mary started to kiss him on the cheek, but he turned his head and her lips brushed his mouth. She blushed and sat down. Nervously, she looked around. The wallpaper was cream-colored. Small blossoming trees climbed from the wainscoting to the ceiling. A glistening crystal chandelier with a dozen candles hung over the oval table. In the center of a lace tablecloth were pink and red flowers.

"Are you starting to feel at home?" Charles asked.

"A little different from Ohio, I expect." Julia reached over and stroked her hand.

Maude came in, carrying a large silver tray. She put it down on the buffet, then set a china plate in front of each of them. There were eggs, ham, and a white mixture unfamiliar to Mary.

"What do the ladies have planned for today?" Charles asked.

"The dressmaker is coming this morning. We must outfit Christabel for the holidays. Christabel dear . . ."

Mary realized Julia was speaking to her.

"Is anything wrong? You look so startled."

Mary shook her head.

"Well, I hope your mama will approve our choices. She
has put you in my hands, and I shall dress you like the
little doll you are. Isn't she a doll, Charles?"

"Absolutely. But, my dear Julia, you must not make a
plaything of her." Charles reached over and lightly
pinched Mary's cheek. "Christabel is, after all, a young
woman."

"I am aware of that, Charles. I simply meant I shall not
dress her in the elegant, stiff clothes that are the cages of
the fashionable. My niece shall remain unfettered."

"Sounds like a good theme for your next speech at that
suffragette group you attend." Charles winked at Mary.

"Don't make fun of me, Charles." Julia shook her finger
at him. "My sister wanted Christabel introduced to a more
sophisticated society. That is why she sent her East. I shall
undertake her education with pleasure."

"Your Aunt Julia will have you dressed like an angel,
but protesting like the devil." Charles laughed.

"Since sister Eleanor saw fit to name Christabel for a
Coleridge heroine, perhaps our niece is destined to be a
Romantic."

Mary was having a difficult time following the conversation. She was aware that she was dreaming, and that in
the dream her name was Christabel. She was the niece of

Charles and Julia. They were talking about her but teasing each other.

"Would you like to go into the city this afternoon?" Charles was speaking directly to Mary. "Roller-skating is the new fad. A nice rink has just opened near Grand Central Station."

"I don't know how to roller-skate," Mary said, the words coming out on one hurried breath.

"Don't worry. They will have instructors." Charles leaned closer. "And I will see that you don't fall down."

"It should be amusing," Julia said.

"You may simply want to observe, darling. I believe it's rather strenuous."

Julia frowned. "I am really quite strong. I find your overprotectiveness somewhat tiresome, Charles dear. Now, Christabel, finish your eggs. They will give you energy for this exhausting roller-skating."

Mary was surprised that she could taste the food. It was delicious.

A noise from the front hall startled her. "What was that?" she asked.

"I beg your pardon?" Julia looked at her, eyebrows raised.

There was a voice. Mary struggled to hear. It sounded like Annie, but it was too faint for her to tell.

"Maude, please answer the door," Charles said.

Mary could still hear Annie's voice. She looked at Charles and Julia. They seemed oblivious.

Maude came back in. "Miss Moriarty is here, ma'am."

"Show her upstairs to the sewing room, please, Maude."

And then they were standing in the hall on the second floor in front of Brian's room. Julia was talking to a round, freckle-faced woman of middle age.

Mary could hear another voice close by, a deeper one.

"Christabel?" Julia touched her shoulder. "Is something wrong?"

"No. No," Mary said quickly.

"Then stop jumping about, dear. Miss Moriarty has a sample she wants you to try on."

Inside the room were dressmaker forms, a long table, and a large sewing machine with a wheel and treadle.

"And if it fits, Miss Christabel might be wearing it for Thanksgiving." Miss Moriarty had a heavy Irish brogue. She held up a long-sleeved brown velvet dress. "Try it on, lass."

Mary unbuttoned her high-necked white blouse, and let her plain gray skirt slide down around her ankles.

A door was slamming. Someone was calling a name, over and over, shutting out Julia's voice, drowning Miss Moriarty's comments. And then the two women were gone, and Mary was trying to find them.

She blinked and rubbed her eyes. She was in the tower, standing by her bed.

She glanced down at the floor, expecting to see the gray skirt. Her bare white feet stuck out from beneath her blue-and-white flannel nightgown.

She ran down the stairs to Brian's room and looked in disbelief at the bunk beds, the toys scattered on the floor.

"What are you looking for?" Brian asked.

She stared at him.

"You sure are hard to wake up," he said. "Your father called you. My mother called you. I called you about a hundred times." He stared back at her. "Whatsa matter?" he asked.

Mary picked up a Lego construction and threw it against the wall. She turned and rushed from the room.

"If Mike weren't coming, I'd tell on you," she heard Brian call after her.

Chapter 12

Mary sat hunched over the breakfast table, staring at her plate. She had to find a way out of working on the trail with Brian and Mike. Otherwise, she would miss the day with Charles and Julia.

Her dreams were in sync with the past. If she dreamed at night, it was night also. If she dreamed in the morning, she found herself transported to another morning. Transported—that was the word for the way she felt.

"I made extra sandwiches." Annie's voice intruded on her thoughts. "I'll bet that rugged young man has a hearty appetite. I was behind a boy in Neilsen's the other day, and he had two full trays of food. I thought he was with someone until I sat at the next table. He

∽ 115

cleaned them both up as if he were a vacuum cleaner."
Annie was busily filling a knapsack.

Christabel. What a strange name, Mary thought. It
was like music.

"Mo-om, have you tried to lift this thing?" Brian pre-
tended he was going to collapse under the weight of the
lunch. Mary realized he was clowning for her benefit,
but she did not react. She was still mad at him for
waking her.

"We're going to the Metropolitan Museum this afternoon," Mary's father said. "We want to have a little
grown-up time. Mary, you'll look after your brother?"

"I don't need looking after." Brian stuck his lip out.

Mary pushed the eggs around on her plate. They
looked disgusting.

"The children will do just fine," Annie said. "I remember as a kid, I loved it when my parents went out and
I had the house to myself."

"Mary, are you feeling all right?" Her father, chin in
hand, was staring at her.

"Yes, I'm all—I mean, no. I feel a little funny—like
I'm coming down with something."

"Why, John, she's pale as a ghost." Annie put her hand
on Mary's forehead.

They were all staring at her. Mary hung her head. "I
think I'd better stay home today," she said.

"Should we call the doctor?" Annie asked.

"Maybe," her father replied. "She's been sleeping a lot
lately."

"She feels downright clammy," Annie said.

"It might be mono," he answered.

"Please!" Mary got to her feet. "Stop talking about me as if I wasn't here, and stop making such a fuss. I've got some kind of bug, that's all."

"We're just concerned about you, sweetheart," her father said.

"I'll go to bed. By tomorrow I'll be fine."

"Well, I'm going to make an appointment with Dr. Bradley for next week. It won't hurt you to have a checkup."

"Perhaps we'd better stay home today. We can see the exhibit another time," Annie said.

"No way!" Mary was almost in tears. "I'll feel terrible if your day is spoiled."

"Calm down, Mary." Her father laid his hand on her arm.

"You go, okay?" Mary pleaded. "If I'm not feeling better by tomorrow, I'll see Dr. Bradley. How's that?"

"What about me? Can I still go with Mike?" Brian asked.

"Of course you can," Annie said. "He's going to be disappointed Mary's sick. You go along and help him."

"You're sure you won't mind being here alone?" Mary's father squeezed her wrist.

"I'll be fine."

Mary had the excuse she needed. She pushed back from the table. According to the clock over the stove, barely an hour had gone by. Surely the dressmaker would still be there with Julia.

Mary did not undress but lay down on top of her

white chenille bedspread. The material was rough against her hot cheek, and she turned down the top and put her head on the cotton pillowcase. It felt cool and good.

The sun shone through the window, the shadow of the panes making a pattern of bars across her and the bed. She closed her eyes and pictured her Christabel self spinning. Her hair streamed out behind her, and her skirt made circles that were fuller and fuller, twirling Mary through space and time.

And then she was in Brian's room. The toys and bunk beds were gone.

"What do you think of it, love? You've been so very quiet and dreamy. This will be your dress for the Christ-mas ball."

There was an oval mirror on a stand, and Mary looked at her reflection, which was somewhat distorted. She was wearing an emerald green silk gown that shimmered in the wavy glass.

Mary stroked the material. "It's beautiful. I feel like Scarlett O'Hara."

"Is that a friend back home?" Julia asked. "I did not know the Irish had settled in Ohio."

"No. No." Mary realized she had blundered. Gone with the Wind *had not been written yet. "Just a charac-ter in a story." To forestall further questions, Mary ex-cused herself. The next room should be the bathroom she shared with Brian. She was curious and a little apprehen-*

118 ∽

sive. If they did not have running water, what was she to do?

She stood in the doorway and looked around. A water tank over the toilet was suspended from the wall near the ceiling and had a long pull cord. The tub was enclosed in wood, and a beautiful old mirror hung over a pedestal sink.

"Mary! Mary-Mary!"

It sounded like Brian calling, but she would not listen. She shut out the voice and walked out the bathroom door. She should have been in the hall, but she was not.

"That's a perfectly suitable traveling costume," Julia said.

Mary looked down bewildered. The green dress was gone. Instead, she was wearing a suit. The jacket had wide lapels, and the blouse had a black bow at the neck. The skirt barely touched the top of her shoes.

"Here comes our locomotive," Charles announced as a train whistle sounded in the distance. Mary shivered, without knowing why. She was standing on the platform of the train station between Charles and Julia. The sun was bright. There was no reason for her chill.

"Hello." Charles shook hands with two gentleman who had approached. One was considerably older than the other. "Good to see you, Pinkham," he said to Charles. "I see you have two plays running simultaneously. Very impressive. Very."

"Thank you, Peter. That's quite a compliment coming from you. One will be closing anyday now, however."

"To be replaced by the one you are writing," Julia said.

So that was what Charles did up in their room, Mary thought. He wrote plays. Successful plays. She looked at him adoringly.

"I do not believe you have met our niece." Charles turned to Mary. "Christabel dear, may I present our neighbors? This is Mr. Peter Hammond and his son, Matthew. Mr. Hammond. Matthew. I have the honor of presenting Miss Kirkland."

The gentlemen bowed to her in turn and tipped their hats. "Your given name is Christabel? That is quite unusual, Miss Kirkland," the older man offered.

"You know the Coleridge poem?" Julia asked. "My sister is very fond of the Romantic poets. She named Christabel for the beautiful, fairylike creature of the poem."

"I'm not a reader of poetry." The younger man spoke up. "But I would say Miss Kirkland is fairly named."

"How gallant, Matthew," Julia said.

Mary was grateful that she was too cold to blush. She looked down the track. The train was not in view.

"It's a fine poem." Julia filled the silence. "It goes something like this:

> "It was a lovely sight to see
> The lady Christabel, when she
> Was praying at the old oak tree."

She stopped and smiled.

"Bravo, darling. Do go on," Charles urged.

120 ∽

"Let me see." Julia put a gloved hand to her chin and briefly narrowed her eyes in thought. "Ah, yes.

"Amid the jagged shadows
Of mossy leafless boughs,
Kneeling in the moonlight,
To make her gentle vows."

"You speak that so well, Mrs. Pinkham," Peter Hammond said. "You could be as big a celebrity as your husband if he put you in his plays."

"Why, Mr. Hammond, how charming." Julia smiled at him.

Then the air was filled with the sound of the train. The hooting of the whistle grew louder as the train drew nearer. The bell clanged and clanged, hurting Mary's ears. The sounds overwhelmed her, pressed in on her, awakening her old fears. She turned to Charles, as the hissing steam enveloped him, blotting him out, and the train slid to a stop. "Charles!" She reached out for him . . .

. . . and found they were in a large room where painted ivy climbed and twisted over white walls. The noise was not the train but notes sounded on a piano and the rumbling of roller skates on the wooden floor. "Charming. Charming. Charming." Charles threw his head back and laughed happily. They were on skates, waltzing in time to the piano. Mary's feet were moving of their own volition. She took a deep breath.

"You are a natural, niece darling," Charles said. "I have never enjoyed skating as much."

As they whirled and dipped, Mary caught a glimpse of Julia watching from the sidelines. She was not smiling.

The tempo of the music increased. Mary was propelled backward rapidly, her skates flying in rhythmic thrusts behind her. Then she was side by side with Charles, swinging in an arc, and whirling in large circles down the very center of the room. The faces of the skaters seemed to fly by, though it was she and Charles who were in flight, going faster and faster until they seemed not to be touching the ground, themselves now spinning in orbit about the crowded floor. And the music stopped. Mary fell against Charles, who caught her, then held her fast. They were both laughing and gasping for breath.

Julia met them as they came off the floor. "You were being a bit reckless, I think, darling," she said. "I beg you to remember, Christabel lacks experience."

"But she is a marvelous skater. What movement! What grace! You must have seen."

"I certainly did see," Julia said, lips tight. "I have been watching for the better part of an hour."

"Sorry, dear." Charles put his arm around Julia. "I hadn't meant to neglect you. It's just that these athletic pursuits aren't exactly your forte—"

Julia pulled away from him. "I might benefit from your instruction."

"I tell you what. Christabel shall take one of your hands, and I shall take the other—"

122 ∾

"Mary!" Her shoulder was being shaken and she reached desperately for Julia's hand.

"Come on!"

Mary tried to pull away. The shaking continued.

"Aren't you ever going to wake up?"

She opened her eyes. Brian was standing over her, and she was clutching the pillow, scrunched down on her bed.

"You've been sleeping all day. I'm lonely."

Chapter 13

English was the last class of the morning and the last class of this short Thanksgiving week. School would be out at noon. Mary could hardly wait. After school she was going to see Mr. Gray again. She had been visiting him every week. She would get him talking about Victorian times. Maybe today he . . .

A hand dropped a blue test booklet on top of her notebook, interrupting Mary's thoughts.

"See me after school," Ms. Martinez said quietly.

Mary looked up at her and nodded.

When the teacher moved down the aisle, Mary opened the cover of the booklet. 42! The numbers were in red at the top of the page and circled. Next to them, Ms. Martinez had drawn a face with mouth turned down. "What happened?" was her only written comment.

Mary had failed the test on *The Odyssey*. She had never even finished reading the book.

She put her elbow on the desk and covered her face with her hand. She was aware that questions were being asked and answers given. If she continued to look down, Ms. Martinez would probably leave her alone.

Tests didn't matter, Mary told herself. Pretty soon she'd be at the Historical Society. She had asked Mr. Gray to look up people who had owned her house in Victorian times. She wanted to find out just when Charles and Julia Pinkham had lived there.

The bell rang and Mary jumped up.

"Anybody need a ride?" Mike Bell was in front of the room. He addressed the question to the group, but he was looking at Mary.

Ms. Martinez laughed. "You must have turned sixteen recently, Mike. Biggest day of a sophomore's life."

"Right." He held up his driver's license. "I'm legal."

Neil slapped him on the back. Others yelled congratulations.

Mary moved across the row to the other side of the room, intending to avoid the knot of students surrounding Mike.

"Don't forget to stay, Mary," Ms. Martinez called.

Mary grimaced.

She had been avoiding the teacher ever since the deadline for her topic had passed. Now Mary was going to have to really concentrate and come up with something.

"Come on into my office." Ms. Martinez led the way

across the hall and through the English and social studies learning center to her small enclosure.

"I want you to see this." She handed Mary a rectangular pink slip of paper. It was a progress report.

The words seemed to blur and run together as Mary stared at them. She blinked, squinted her eyes, and read:

Mary has not appeared at appointments concerning a critical independent study. Additionally, she seems ill prepared for class. She has failed a major test. Her oral participation grade has gone from B to F. Please call to arrange a meeting with Mary, her guidance counselor, and me.

Alicia Martinez

"I'm sending that to your parents, Mary, and I don't want you taken by surprise. You must realize you are failing English."

The paper fell out of Mary's hand and floated down to the floor as she watched it. "I'm failing?"

"The independent studies are a major part of the grade. Everyone else has finished the research and has started a first draft. You haven't even chosen a topic," Ms. Martinez said.

"I'm working on it." Mary bit her lip.

"I've talked to Mrs. Bermingham. She says you've only been to the library once."

"But I've been going to the Historical Society. You can call and ask Mr. Gray."

"What have you been doing there, Mary?"

"I've been—learning about Sound Port in Victorian times. I could do a paper on it. I could have that done by the due date."

"I'm afraid I don't see how that relates to English. And it's not just the report. You show no interest in class. I look at you, and you're miles away. Now, if there's something bothering you . . ."

Mary shook her head.

"I've looked at your records. You've always been a straight-A student. Now you're failing. There has to be a reason. I'm going to suggest to your parents that you see Mrs. Rosten."

"Mrs. Rosten?"

"She's a social worker. She's a wonderful person. You will love her, I promise."

"No. No way. Please! I'll make up all the work," Mary pleaded. "See, it's just that I got too involved with this research. I let other things slide. I won't do that anymore."

Ms. Martinez raised her eyebrows. "I can't say the Victorians have fascinated any of my former students. What has appealed so much to you?"

"Lots of stuff. Like the railroads became really important then. And railroad stations . . ."

"Railroad stations?" Ms. Martinez looked over her glasses.

"Or sports," Mary said hurriedly. "They roller-skated, and they had bicycles. You know? Big three-wheeled bicycles." Just yesterday afternoon Charles had given Julia and Christabel such bicycles. They had put Julia in a really good mood. Julia liked it when Charles included her in sports with him and Christabel.

Miss Moriarty's face had been priceless when Julia had asked her to make them bloomers. "Mother of our Lord, what next?" she had said, scandalized. How she and Julia had laughed—not in front of her, of course.

"Mary?"

She jerked back to Ms. Martinez's office. "Yes?"

"What is so funny?"

"Funny?"

"You laughed out loud."

"Oh!" Mary was flustered. "The bicycles, I guess. You'd have to see them. I mean, the pictures of them."

The teacher was really looking at her strangely now. She would have to be more careful. Ms. Martinez already wanted to send her to a shrink.

"This seems a very long way from English, Mary. I'm sorry you've wasted so much time on this research. And I'm afraid I still don't understand the fascination."

"Local authors!" Mary said loudly. The topic had meant nothing when Mrs. Bermingham had suggested it. Now that she had learned that Charles wrote plays, it was perfect!

"I beg your pardon?"

"I'll do the paper on local authors who lived in Victorian times. That's English, right?"

"Possibly," the teacher said. "Have you read about any authors who wrote here in the Victorian era?"

"Some." Mary had to be careful. "There was one playwright that I'm interested in. Could I, maybe, give some background on the way he lived and then something about his plays?" Her voice rose, excited.

"Hmm." The teacher looked thoughtful. "That approach would allow you to use the research you've done on daily life and still do some analysis that would make it an English paper."

"Oh, yes!" Please let the teacher agree, Mary prayed. She could write about her dreams, and no one would know it. She would have to find copies of his plays. She was sure Mr. Gray could help her.

"I'd need to see an outline," Ms. Martinez said.

"I'll write one over the weekend. I promise."

"All right," the teacher said, although she sounded a little dubious.

"Maybe you don't have to send the progress report?" Mary ventured.

The teacher held up empty hands. "I haven't seen anything on paper."

"Could you just give me until Monday?" It was hard for Mary to beg, but harder to imagine her father reading that progress report. That mustn't happen. Only once in her life had Mary seen her father explode. He had been tricked, taken advantage of by his law partner in Freedom. After a terrible scene, her father had refused to see his former best friend ever again.

Mary leaned toward Ms. Martinez, pleading, "I'll do more than an outline. I'll bring in the whole section describing the playwright's life."

"But I told you. It's not just the report. It's your class participation . . . your homework . . ."

"I'll do all my homework, and I'll pay attention in class from now on. I really will."

"I hate to spoil your holiday . . ." Ms. Martinez struggled with the decision.

Mary swallowed. "Please give me a chance, Ms. Martinez."

Ms. Martinez gave in. "All right, Mary. But I want you to give some thought to a conference with Mrs. Rosten, and I want to see you in this office after school on Monday—with a substantial amount of work. Agreed?"

Mary jumped up. "Thank you." She was almost sobbing with relief. "Oh, thank you!"

"Have a nice Thanksgiving." Ms. Martinez patted her hand.

That had been a close call. Mary thought about it all the way to the Preble-Dickey House. She told herself she really would work all weekend and not let anything get in her way. She felt as if someone had thrown cold water in her face.

Hartley Gray was waiting for her when she arrived. "Have the tea all made," he said. "Let's have it in the library." He led the way to a book-lined room. There was a fire burning in the fireplace.

"Sit right down." He motioned to an easy chair near the fire. He put the tea tray on a table and poured two cups. After he handed one to Mary, he went over to a large desk in front of a window. "Been trying to find who owned your house," he said. "It turns out to be a complicated business. There are sets of books at Town Hall that tell who *bought* property and when. Then there are separate sets that tell who *sold* property and when. Make it a lot easier if they put them in the same volume."

"I'm sorry," Mary said. "I didn't know it would be so much trouble."

"I'm enjoying it, really, but it's going to take some time." Mr. Gray took a slip of paper from the top drawer of the desk. He looked at it through the bottom of his glasses. "Here's what I have so far. In 1897 the house was sold by J. P. Holden. Looking in the other book, I discovered it was bought by a Clarence Smith."

"J. P. Holden?" Mary asked. "Who owned it before him? Did you find out?"

"That's one of the places I ran into trouble." Mr. Gray walked over to Mary and held out the paper. "In 1885 it was sold by an Ezra Ford and purchased by J. Charles Pinkham."

J. Charles Pinkham. Charles had lived in her house in 1885—over a hundred years ago. And she, Christabel, had lived there with him then.

". . . no record of this Pinkham selling it to Holden."

"I'm sorry. What did you say, Mr. Gray?"

"I can't find when this Pinkham sold the house. There could have been another owner in between him and Holden. I'll keep looking."

"Don't bother. Really." Mary forced herself to concentrate on the conversation. She was in a mess, and she needed help.

"Mr. Gray, my teacher wants me to do a report that has more to do with literature. She suggested playwrights. She said there had been"—Mary was feeling her way carefully, trying to give her story credibility—"at least one or two from Sound Port."

"There was an artists' colony," Mr. Gray said. "Some of those fellows did make names for themselves. There was also quite a theatrical community here in the last century—probably what your teacher is talking about. Edwin Booth lived here."

Oh, no, Mary thought. He was going to suggest someone other than Charles.

"He was a well-known actor. Got overshadowed by his brother, John Wilkes Booth. He was the bad actor who shot Abraham Lincoln."

"I couldn't use him, then," Mary said quickly. "It has to be a playwright. Is there any way to find out what playwrights lived here in the 1880s, say?"

"Certainly. That should be easy. I'll rustle around here and see what I learn, and I'll give the Dramatists Guild a call. I'll get on it this afternoon."

"I don't know how to thank you. I'm in real trouble over this report."

"A lovely girl like you in trouble? Well, we can't have that. And you don't need to thank me. Your visits are thank-you enough."

"I like to come here. You know an awful lot."

"Scenes flash through my mind, and voices chatter away their old stories. I don't want to keep them inside like I'm a dead-end street. You're a good listener."

Mary had a sudden urge to tell him that there were scenes in her mind, too. There were voices in her dreams. He was smiling at her, almost the way Gramps used to smile. She wished she were a little girl who could curl up on his lap and tell him her secret.

But, of course, she couldn't.

She finished the rest of her tea and said goodbye to Mr. Gray.

Chapter 14

It was a warm day for late November, and Mary had chosen to walk home rather than wait for her father. When she opened the front door, she found Annie once again in the hall. A large portion of the wall had been stripped, exposing a crimson-and-green paisley design. Mary put out her hand and touched it. Though the paper was streaked with dried paste, cracked and faded, she recognized it.

". . . white as a sheet . . . feel all right? . . . good thing it's vacation." She became aware Annie was talking to her. "A little rest and fresh air will do you good. What do you think? I'm down to an early layer. I like this paper. If I can duplicate it, I'll do the hall in it."

Annie came into focus. "Do the hall in this paper?" Mary echoed.

"Wouldn't it be just *wonderful* to have the real thing? Well, not the real thing, of course. A reproduction. I'm going into New York on Friday to meet with Donna Molyneux. She's a fabulous decorator. I've sent her lots of clients, so she's going to get me into all the showrooms. I want to have this hall done by Christmas. But what decisions . . . furniture, rugs . . ."

"Can I go with you?"

Annie looked surprised. "To the city to look at furnishings? If you want to. By all means. I'd love to have you." She smiled happily. "I didn't know you were interested. I left that book of wallpaper in your room and drapery samples for those cold, bare windows. You never said a word."

"I am interested," Mary said. With Annie's unwitting help, she would take the house back to its original state. It would be sort of like a monument to Charles and Julia.

"This hall is so big I'll probably have to sell two houses to furnish it," Annie said. "I'm about to close a deal on the old Warner place. You would not believe that this couple who thought they wanted a squeaky-clean modern house with lots of glass would settle on a farmhouse built in 1825 and inhabited by squirrels and various other small wild beasties. That's one problem we no longer have here. At least now we are the only tenants . . ."

Not exactly, Mary thought to herself, and smiled at her little unspoken joke.

"No more nests in the walls or hives in the attic,"

Annie was going on. "We're the busy bees. I'll call Donna and tell her you're coming to New York with me. That will be *fab*-ulous. You can help me decide what to put in here."

"I've done some research," Mary said, "for an English paper on the Victorians. There might have been a piece of furniture right about there." She pointed to a space to the right of the front doors. "A tall thin thing with hooks to hold hats. Can we find something like that?"

"They were called hat trees," Annie replied. "Well, sure. One would look great there. We could cover it with straw hats. You know the kind, with long ribbons and pretty flowers. It would be just like a still life in that corner."

"What about a table for here?" Mary walked over to the wall opposite the staircase. "And two chairs? You could put a dish on the table for calling cards. Over it, you could put a big mirror, with a fancy frame." Mary wondered if she were saying too much and stopped abruptly. "I've seen pictures like that," she said.

"Calling cards? Who would we have?" Annie laughed. "The plumber and the electrician could leave theirs, I suppose. They are here more than any other callers. But guess what? We are going to have a party. I want to have it New Year's Eve, but your father doesn't want people driving that night. He thinks it's dangerous. So we're going to have it on the eve of New Year's Eve."

"This is news to me," Mary said.

"We just thought of it. You can invite that adorable

boy who is practically chopping down the forest to get your attention."

Mary opened her mouth to protest, but Annie was off on another subject. Anyway, it wouldn't hurt to invite Mike. Maybe he'd come . . . maybe not . . .

"I want to have the house in great shape. I'm so glad you're going to help! Oh, my goodness—" Annie looked at her watch. "I'm going to be late. I have to meet my clients at the bank in half an hour, and I'm not even dressed yet."

"Where's Brian?" Mary asked.

"His school is on a field trip. He won't be back until six. Your dad's going to pick him up," Annie said.

It was a good time to get started on her paper, Mary decided. Usually she went to her room to do her homework, but that was sometimes too much of a temptation. With no one home to bother her, she could work downstairs on the sun porch.

Her father had put up the glass windows against the coming winter, and the sun shining through them was warm and welcome. She sat on the glider, feet tucked under her, a pad of lined paper and a pencil in her hands. "A Writer in Victorian Times," Mary wrote in the center of the top line. She chewed on her pencil, trying to think of a way to begin.

"The life of a writer in Victorian times was a fulfilling one. Take Charles Pinkham. He lived in a large house, which though it lacked today's conveniences was . . ." What? Well run? Uh-huh, but that wasn't quite it. *Gracious.* Satisfied, she wrote down the word.

"This was partially due to having servants." Mary made a face, thinking of dour Maude, whose lip seemed to curl down whenever she spoke to Christabel.

She read over what she had written. What a dull way to begin a paper, she thought. And Charles was anything but dull. She crossed out the sentences and started over. "Six feet tall, with dark curly hair and laughing brown eyes, the playwright is handsome. He has many interests. He is a sensational roller skater, a fabulous dancer, an amateur magician, among other things. Though he is in his thirties, he acts younger."

Stuck again, Mary closed her eyes. She would not dream, she promised herself. She would just picture him—and Julia.

The sun was warm on her face. It reminded Mary of the heat from the fireplace in Riverview. Just last evening, she had sat on a footstool, her head resting against Charles's knee while Julia coached her. She was teaching Mary the poem for which Christabel was named.

" 'It was a lovely sight to see,' " Julia had quoted, and Mary had echoed the line. " 'The lady Christabel, when she,' " continued Julia, and Mary had repeated it. " 'Was praying at the old oak tree.' "

"Wait!" Charles had interrupted. "I have a new version. It goes like this: It is a lovely sight to see, My lady Christabel when she is resting on her uncle's knee."

"Do sit up, Christabel," Julia had said. "Mind your posture. And, Charles, I wish you would not be quite

138 ✑

such a distraction." The firelight cast shadows that flickered on the wall. Charles had stood up abruptly and walked over to the fire, where he rubbed his hands in front of it. His enormous shadow seemed to dominate the room, stretching across the floor and up the wall in a peculiar slant.

There had been a strange silence in the room, and then an odd ringing noise.

"Ah, the telephone," Charles said, crossing the room. Maude appeared at the door. "I'll get it, Maude," he said.

He spoke briefly on the telephone. "The Maynards will come for Thanksgiving," he said, when he had hung up. "They want us for their salon on Sunday. With Christabel, of course. No one can get enough of our charming young relative. I swear our invitations have doubled."

"Hardly, Charles. It is you, not Christabel, who is lionized," Julia said. "Your uncle flatters you, Christabel. He is much sought after because of the success of his plays. You will enjoy the parties, however. Like satellite moons, you and I shall shine in his reflected glow."

"Nonsense. You are much too modest, Julia dear. I shall be the envy of all the men as I escort my two beauties."

Rap! Rap! Rap! Mary jumped as someone tapped loudly on the window behind her head. She turned to see Mike Bell grinning at her. He walked around the corner to the outside door. She got up and opened it.

"Hope I didn't scare you, Mary Barrone." His eyes crinkled as he smiled at her.

"You just startled me. It's all right." Mary smiled back, feeling more like Christabel than herself.

"C'mon out and take a look at this trail. Here I am, slaving away, and you never show up when I'm around."

"I'll get my jacket," Mary said.

Mike had cleared a path about two feet wide beginning at the place in the wall where the stones had fallen away. It followed briefly the route Mary and Brian had been accustomed to taking, then veered off to the left, in the opposite direction from the river and station. Only a few leaves clung to the trees, and the sun shone brightly.

"What do you think?" Mike asked. "You got a clear shot now to a good trail."

"It's a lot easier walking," Mary said. Just then she stumbled over a root in the ground. Mike caught her with one hand and put his arm around her to steady her.

"Sure is." He laughed.

"I wasn't looking where I was going." Mary straightened up. He kept his hand on her shoulder as they resumed their walk. It was a light pressure, but Mary felt heat radiating through her jacket.

They came to a wider trail that was part of the system in the nature preserve. "This way." Mike steered her to the right. The trail was wide and went up an incline. Logs had been placed every few feet. "Keeps the trail from washing out in the spring thaw," he explained. At the top of the hill, the trail split. A square of orange wood was nailed on a tree to their left. "The orange route actually makes a circle and comes out at the nature

140 ⌒

preserve cabin," Mike told her, "but we're not going that way. I have a surprise for you."

They continued on to the right, walking along a ridge for about a quarter of a mile, until the path descended abruptly into a ravine. Mike went ahead, stopping every few feet to reach back and give Mary a hand as she scrambled down the loose gravel. When they reached the bottom, Mike held on to her hand as they followed, single file, a narrow trail, where branches hung down and bushes caught at their jeans. "Need to do a little work here," Mike said.

He held back a branch and pulled her past it. "This is it," he said.

They were in a holly grove. The glossy green leaves glistened in the sunshine, and the red berries were thick and lush. Some of the trees were gigantic. Mary had always thought of holly as growing on bushes, but many of these trees soared thirty feet in the air.

"It's beautiful!" Mary shook her head in wonder. "I've never seen anything like it."

"I thought you'd like it. C'mon, we'll walk around." The ground was smooth, and there were open spaces between the trees. "The grove covers a couple of acres," Mike said. "Look at all the varieties. See. There are lots of different shades of green."

"It's like being in a Christmas wonderland," Mary said. "I almost expect sugarplum fairies to dance out from behind the trees."

"It should be snowing, and then it would be perfect," Mike said. "Can't you imagine standing here in the quiet of a snowfall? Will you come back with me when it snows, Mary Barrone?" He looked into her eyes. She felt trembly and wanted to look away but somehow couldn't.

She swallowed and nodded. "Yes."

"I can't think of any other girl I'd want to come here with," Mike said. "There's something about you . . ." He squinted at her, as if he were trying to figure something out. "I don't know . . . strange isn't exactly the right word . . ."

"Weird, maybe?" Mary said. She was surprised to find she could joke. The way Mike was talking to her made her feel unbearably tense—tense and tingly.

"No. No. No. Deep and quiet. That make any sense? It's like, there can be all this hubbub around you, and you're there in the center with a stillness. Ah, I'm not very good at this. You've seen lilies on ponds? Well, you're like a delicate pink flower, floating on dark, quiet water."

"That sounds like poetry," she said.

"Yeah? Don't tell anyone, but I like poetry. I like the sounds of words and hearing the right words together. But you can't give it away too much in school. It doesn't go with the jock image."

"Have you ever read Coleridge?"

"He wrote the poem about the old guy who couldn't stop telling his story. Right? The Ancient Mariner?"

Mary nodded. "He also wrote a poem called 'Christabel.' That's my favorite:

> *"It was a lovely sight to see*
> *The lady Christabel, when she*
> *Was praying at the old oak tree.*
> *Amid the jagged shadows*
> *Of mossy leafless boughs,*
> *Kneeling in the moonlight,*
> *To make her gentle vows . . .*

"Oh, what am I doing?" Mary said, blushing. "I guess you shouldn't have told me you like poetry."

"Hey, don't stop. That's great stuff. I could see it. The shadows. The moonlight. What's she doing out there alone in the night, though?"

"I don't know. I'm just learning the poem, and I haven't gotten that far."

"When you find you, will you tell me?"

"Perhaps when we come back in the snow," Mary said, and realized that for the first time in her life, she was flirting.

Chapter 15

~~~~~~

The telephone rang while they were having dinner. "It's for you, Mary. A man." Annie covered the receiver and handed Mary the phone. "Not that darling boy, though. Someone older."

"Hello?"

"Mary? It's Hartley Gray. I hope I'm not bothering you, but I couldn't wait to tell you what I found out."

"It's no bother."

"You're not going to believe this, but there *was* a playwright named Pinkham. Charles Pinkham. Wouldn't it beat all if it was the same Pinkham who lived in your house?"

Mary could hardly believe her luck. Mr. Gray had discovered exactly what she had hoped he would. "That's fantastic," she said.

"The dates match. This fellow was writing plays at the same time a J. Charles Pinkham lived where you do now. I'm betting they're the same man."

"Charles Pinkham." Mary liked saying his name aloud. "What a wonderful coincidence."

"Here's the reference. From *The Village Gazette*—July, 1885: 'The Players, a New York club for actors, playwrights, and prominent businessmen, was conceived by Edwin Booth and Charles Pinkham while guests of Commander Benedict on his yacht, *Oneida*. The cruise celebrated the success of Booth in Pinkham's hit play *The General.*' "

"Do you think that play would be in the library?"

"If not, we can probably get a copy from the Dramatists Guild in New York."

"Mr. Gray, I really appreciate this."

"I like having a new project. Why don't you stop by on Monday. I'll show you the article and anything else I manage to find."

"Okay. Thanks a lot."

"Have a nice Thanksgiving, Mary."

"You too."

"Well, Mary," Annie said as Mary hung up the receiver. "You look like the cat who ate the canary. That's a disgusting expression, isn't it? But you look awfully pleased."

"That was someone from the Historical Society. He has stuff for my English report."

"I hated writing papers when I was in school," Annie said. "But give me a paintbrush or clay, and I was happy as a clam. Now, there's another dumb expression. What do clams have to be happy about? I hope I'm not reincarnated as a shellfish."

"You won't be," Brian said. "You'll come back as something that talks a lot."

"Hey, Sam," Mary's father said, "I hope you are not going to spend the weekend in your room with your nose in a book. We hardly see you anymore."

It was going to be a problem. Mary wanted to have Thanksgiving with Charles and Julia, but she couldn't be in two places at once. And if she was caught sleeping again, they would drag her to the doctor.

"What time are we having dinner?" Mary asked.

"Not before four," her father said. "Annie bought such a big turkey I'd have to get up in the middle of the night to put it in the oven if we ate any earlier."

"It's our first Thanksgiving as a family," Annie said. "If they had a fifty-pound turkey, I would have bought it to celebrate."

"As it is, we'll be eating turkey until Christmas."

"I'm very creative with leftovers, John. We'll have turkey pie and turkey croquettes and—"

"Please not turkey quee-chee!" Brian made a face. "Last year when Ma had food left over, she put it in a quee-chee."

"What's a quee-chee?" his stepfather asked.

Annie managed to stop laughing to explain. "Quiche. Brian, I've told you a hundred times. It's quiche, not quee-chee."

Brian shrugged. "Anyway, we had quee-chees all the time."

"What are we having with the turkey?" Mary asked.

"Despite what Brian says, I'm very old-fashioned. We'll have a traditional dinner—mashed potatoes, carrots, creamed onions, cranberry sauce, turnips—"

"Turnips! Know what I heard in school? The vegetables for lunch today will be lettuce, turn-up, and pea." Brian giggled.

"Brian, that's rude!" Annie scolded.

"Perfect fifth-grade humor. That's the way boys talk." Mary's father sounded almost pleased.

"Not to their parents," Annie said. "That's strictly for the washroom. I wonder why girls don't tell dirty jokes?"

Before Annie could get sidetracked, Mary spoke up. "I'll help you with the vegetables in the morning."

"You promised we'd take a walk to . . ." Brian began, but Mary gave him a warning look. He had been pestering her to go back to the train station, and until now, she had resisted. She hated to see it in its present state. To make up for not working with him and Mike on the trail, she had finally given in, but she had made him promise again to keep it a secret.

"We'll take a walk," she said quickly, "and then I'll help your mother." She looked at her father. "But I do need some time to work on my paper. From like one to four. That okay?"

"I don't see why you can't study on Friday instead of Thanksgiving Day," he said.

"Friday I'm going into New York with Annie."

"Well, good!" The frown disappeared and he smiled happily. "Do a little work tomorrow if you really must."

John got to his feet, leaned over and kissed the top of Mary's head. "I am proud of you, Sam, for being such a dedicated A-plus, number one student, you know."

Mary winced and slid out of her chair, ducking away from her father. "I'll do the dishes," she said.

In bed, she debated. She had escaped to her room later than usual. If she dreamed herself into the past, Charles and Julia might be asleep. She did not want to wander around alone in the house in the night. No, she would see them tomorrow.

She closed her eyes and pictured Mike Bell, grinning at her as he had that afternoon. He reached out and took her hand. Mary remembered how that had felt. He had looked into her eyes and she could hear her heart beating. She had thought he might kiss her.

". . . come back with me when it snows, Mary Barrone?" The way he said her name pleased her. Not just Mary. Mary Barrone. She could see the holly grove in the snow. Gentle white flakes would land on them and melt. Mike would have his arm around her, and she would rest her head against his shoulder.

Mary snuggled down into the pillow.

Early morning light streamed into her room, and Mary woke to a dream unbidden. She watched her dream body spinning in the middle of the room. Slowly at first, then faster and faster, it twirled round and round. Her feet were not touching the floor, and her skirt flared out, brushing the walls as she spun around the perimeter of the room. Mary felt dizzy and confused.

The kitchen was filled with strong, sweet smells. Three steaming pies sat on a sideboard. Maude, in a black apron, stood at a center butcher block, chopping onions. "What are you wanting here, miss?" she asked Mary.

"Why . . . uh . . . some water?"

"You know where the pump is." Maude gestured to the sink. "I'm not waiting on you. Seems to me you want more than water." This last was muttered.

"I beg your pardon?"

"I know your kind. Butter wouldn't melt in your mouth, would it?"

Mary felt tears come to her eyes. Why did this woman hate her so?

"Is everything coming along all right?" Julia came into the kitchen.

"Pies are done. Bread's in. I'm on the stuffing now," Maude said.

"Why, Christabel, whatever is wrong? Are you crying?"

Maude was glaring at Mary, hands on hips, daring her to tell.

"No. It's—the onions. They make my eyes run."

Maude turned away, a satisfied smile on her face. "Dinner at two, is it, ma'am?"

"Yes. There will be twelve of us. I'm sure I told you that. Come along, Christabel. A little fresh air will be good for us."

Then, bundled up in coats, they were walking down a

wagon path that Mary had not seen before. Dead brown grass topped the center mound between two frozen ruts.

"Do you look forward to seeing Matthew Hammond again?" Julia's voice was light and teasing. "I think he is quite smitten with you."

"We met at the train station, right?" Mary said cautiously.

"You sly one. Of course you met there. Are you trying to pretend you have forgotten his daily calls? It is true you have managed to be out frequently when he arrives, but you must have a drawerful of his cards by now."

"Not quite," Mary replied.

"I think you are very sensible not to encourage him too much. There will be many other young men at our Christmas ball, and it is best that you are quite unattached. However, we always have the Hammonds for Thanksgiving, so he will be with us today. From the pink of your complexion, dear Christabel, I may take it you will not mind." Julia laughed and pinched Mary's cheek.

They were at the top of an incline, and Julia led Mary down a smaller path that branched to the right.

"I want to show you something," Julia said.

They came out into a slanting meadow dotted with small bushes. "I had these planted for Charles on his last birthday."

"What are they?"

"Holly. This is the Happy Birthday Holly Grove." The leaves were glossy green but sparse and there were tiny red berries. "I hope they are going to live," Julia said. "I wanted to give Charles something that would grow and be

beautiful." She took Mary's hand and pulled her down to sit on a large, flat-topped rock. They tucked skirts and petticoats around their legs and pulled collars up around their necks.

"Oh, it's just wonderful!" Mary said. "The trees reach up to the sky!"

"Not quite." Julia looked puzzled. "But I hope they will grow well," she said. "It is all I seem to be able to give my husband for posterity."

At that moment a cloud edged over the sun, and Julia's face darkened in shadow.

"What do you mean?" Mary asked.

"Surely you understand. I am thirty-two and have no children."

"Oh." Mary hated to see Julia unhappy. "Lots of women have babies in their thirties—"

"At any rate," Julia interrupted, "we have you for a time. Charles is quite taken with you."

In the distance, a thin, lonely train whistle blew to them across the woods, like an echo of Mary's old fears.

Chapter 16

The smells wafting up the stairs were familiar.
Mary had showered and put on khakis, and in the mirror
her ordinary, everyday face had looked back at her. The
smells, however, were exactly those of her dream. She
hurried down to the kitchen.

"Oh, it's you!" she blurted out, relieved to see Annie,
not Maude, stirring something on the stove.

"Well, of course, it's me." Annie laughed. "You didn't
expect to find your father out here cooking all of
Thanksgiving dinner, did you? He put the turkey in at
the crack of dawn. He's resting. We're on our own for
breakfast. Grab some cereal or a muffin."

Brian was buttering toast, and Annie chattered on
while Mary and Brian ate. Mary kept thinking about

Maude. Maybe she should have told Julia what the woman had said to Christabel. And the way she had looked at her, so cold and mean—involuntarily, Mary shivered.

"Someone walk over your grave?" Annie glanced over at her. "Don't look so startled. It's just an expression. Rather a morbid one, now that I think of it."

"She would like to walk over my grave."

"Who?" Annie dropped the spoon on the stove and came over to Mary. "What are you talking about, Mary?"

"I'm sorry. I was thinking about . . . just . . . uh . . ." She put her hand over her face. "Forget it."

"That's a very serious accusation," Annie said. "That someone would want to walk on your grave. It makes me sad that you would even think that. Why, it's out of the question. But, if someone is being terrible to you, I want to know—"

"Please, just forget it," Mary repeated. "I didn't know what I was saying." She got up quickly from the table. "You ready, Brian? What can we take for snacks?" Mary asked Annie, hoping to divert her.

It worked. Annie rummaged in the closet and came up with packages of crackers and cheese. "And here." She reached in the refrigerator. "Oranges."

Mary hurried Brian, wanting to get away before Annie could ask any more questions. She had slipped again—badly. She would have to concentrate, or she was going to give herself away.

She tried to talk Brian into walking on the new path

and following one of the marked trails, but he was adamant. "You said we could go to the station. You promised."

They came to the clearing in the woods where she had left her bandanna on their first walk. It seemed a lifetime ago.

"There used to be juniper bushes here," she said to Brian.

"What are june-per bushes?"

"They grow low to the ground and have pretty blue berries."

"I never saw those. When did you see them, Mary?"

"A very long time ago."

"Huh?"

"You wouldn't understand. Come on." She led the way to the old train tracks and they climbed up the embankment. She picked up the pace, half expecting to find the station restored. There would be a horse and buggy. Julia and Charles would be on the platform with a lot of people waiting for the train. She would run up and hug them and say, "Oh, am I glad to see you!"

"Who?" Brian came running along by her side. "Who are you talking to?"

She stopped and put her hand to her mouth. "Oh, no," she moaned. What was happening to her? She had to get control of herself. Brian was staring. If she wasn't more careful, both he and Annie were going to think she was crazy. She let her hand drop. "I have something on my mind," she said as calmly as she could. "I guess I was talking to myself because I'm worried."

The glasses magnified his eyes, making them look large and round. "Oh? What?"

"I'm friends with this couple, see?" She had to tell him something. "They have a problem. Well, they can't seem to have a baby, and they feel awful about it."

"So?" Brian shrugged. "Why does that make you talk to yourself?"

"Because they want me to . . . I think they want me to come live with them." With the words came the knowledge it was true.

Brian stared at her, open-mouthed. "That's crazy. You—you can't do that. You have to live with us. Who are they, anyway? Where do they live?"

"Very near here."

"Near *here?*"

"I can't explain it, Brian, and you can't tell anyone about it. Promise?"

Brian frowned and his lips drew in tightly. He didn't answer.

"You have to promise, Brian, or I'll never tell you anything again. I thought we were friends and I could trust you."

"We are." Brian kicked at the path, looking away from Mary. "I'll promise. I will, if you say you're not going to leave us."

Mary chose her words carefully. "I don't intend to leave you."

"Then I promise."

The train station was bleak and cold. "There's nothing to see here," Mary said. "Let's go home."

"I just want to look inside." Brian made his way carefully across the platform.

Mary followed, watching for rotten boards in the stationhouse floor. Brian went in to the little office.

The clock on the wall caught her eye. "I wonder what day it stopped," she said, more to herself than to Brian. He was trying to unwind a spool of tickets and did not answer.

Mr. Gray had said the station was used until sometime in the 1900s. She thought about Charles and Julia. They might have been among the last passengers before the station was closed. She pictured it boarded up and deserted, the clock running down until it finally stopped one day at 2:05.

The idea made her melancholy, and she was quiet on the walk home. Once there, she peeled vegetables as she had promised. Then she went to her room.

They were waiting for her. She could almost feel their presence. She was not aware that she had lain down and closed her eyes.

Immediately she was walking down the stairs, careful not to trip over the full skirts of her dress. Charles and Julia were standing in the front hall looking up at her. Charles leaned over to his wife and whispered. They both laughed. Julia held out her hand to Mary as she reached the hall and twirled her around.

"The dress is perfect," she said. "The high neck is properly demure; yet one sees you are developing into a woman."

156 ✑

"A lovely one at that," Charles said.

"Charles darling, we are quite ready, as you see. Our guests are not expected for half an hour. You have been promising to read us from your play. Would you do that now?"

"Does that appeal, Christabel?" Charles asked.

"Very much," Mary said eagerly.

"All right, then," Charles said, and led the way upstairs.

Mary felt as if she were floating. As Charles opened the door to her tower room, she wondered if she would see her twentieth-century body lying in bed.

But there was the maroon love seat where her bed should be. Mary knelt down on it and looked out the window. In the distance she could see a small slice of the river. That had not changed. The river moved but went nowhere. Mary wondered if time were like that.

"I'll give you background on the play. Then, if you like, we can all read parts."

"Fine," Julia agreed. "Do you have a title yet?"

"A working title. It will probably change. I call it 'Long Distances.' "

He picked up a sheaf of papers next to the typewriter and sat on the edge of the desk. Julia joined Mary on the love seat.

"I hope you're not going to find it too modern. I've been reading this Norwegian fellow, and I think he's on to something with his realism."

"Indeed?"

"I don't think you've read A Doll's House, Julia, but

my play is to be something of a male answer. Ibsen's play," he explained, "shows the plight of modern woman, trapped by conventions and marriage. Mine will show the plight of modern man."

"And what is that plight?" Julia asked.

"The fellow in my play—the leading character—is a man who has always subscribed to modern morality. He is a loving husband, an ambitious and successful business-man, a leader in his prosperous community. He is, in short, a success."

"Many men would like to suffer his—plight—as you call it," Julia said.

"True enough. But in the play, something has made him realize that for everything he has gained, he has paid a price by giving away a bit of his freedom. His profession ties him down, prevents him from seeing the world. His class limits his acquaintances to people just like him."

"And his wife?"

"That is more complicated. You see, she is close to perfect—beautiful, cultured, accomplished. It is only that their marriage has become like a dance—stylish and man-nered. They know all the steps, and they do them beauti-fully, but these steps do not vary. An elegance of form; a lack of passion perhaps."

Mary found the conversation hard to follow. Julia's body had tensed, and she was sitting on the edge of the love seat.

"What has changed him?" Julia asked.

"I'm not sure," he replied. "An emissary from a wider

world awakened him, I think. Perhaps a visitor from the Continent, where the moral code is not as restrictive."

"Missus Pinkham," Maude called up the stairs. "The Hammonds are here."

"Already?" Julia rose. "We did not get to play our parts, I'm sorry to say. I am sure to have given a good interpretation of the wife."

"Julia?" Charles put his hands on her arms, stopping her. "Are you annoyed?" Then he chuckled. "Surely, you don't think— I do not write autobiographically. You know that."

"Of course you don't. I am not annoyed with you. I am just a bit put out that the Hammonds came early and interrupted." She reached back and took Mary's hand. "Mr. Matthew Hammond was eager to see Christabel, no doubt."

"Is that so?" Charles asked. "Do you welcome his attentions, Christabel? Or should I drop some discouraging words to his papa?"

Mary blushed, embarrassed.

"Do hush, Charles," Julia said. "It is appropriate that Christabel have a suitor. As long as she keeps him at a distance."

The Hammonds were in the parlor. They looked different without the tall hats they had worn at the train station. The elder, Peter Hammond, had white hair and sideburns. His son, Matthew, had masses of brown curly hair that extended to the middle of his ears in the front and to the base of his neck in the back.

Peter Hammond presented a bouquet to Julia. "From New York City," he said. "Matthew went in especially to get it."

"Why, Matthew, how sweet!" Julia smiled at him, then handed the flowers to Mary. "Would you arrange these, dear?"

"May I keep you company, Miss Kirkland?" Matthew followed Mary. "The flowers were chosen because they reminded me of you," he said, once they were out of earshot.

"They were?" Mary tried to put distance between them, but seemed unable to move faster.

"Yes. The deep green leaves are the color of your eyes, and the roses—they are called sweetheart roses—are the color of your cheeks." He caught up with Mary and looked down at her. "Especially the color your cheeks are now!"

Maude was at the stove in the kitchen. Face burning and voice unsteady, Mary asked her for a vase.

"Out there." Without turning around, Maude gestured to a small room off the kitchen.

In Sound Port it was the mud room. Here there were cupboards that held assorted vases and a sink in a wooden stand. Mary reached for a vase, but it was too high. Matthew handed it down to her.

He was smiling. "You must not mind if I tease you," he said. "I mean no harm, and you are charming when you blush."

Turning away, she thrust the flowers into the container. Then she hurried ahead of Matthew to the parlor. She looked at him and thought of Mike.

Other guests had arrived. Talk and laughter swirled around her. Charles or Julia was always at her side.

"You must meet our niece, who is with us for the winter."

"Have you met our darling Christabel?"

"Christabel is bringing sunshine to a cold season."

Mary felt as if she were in a play. She said her lines, but the words were someone else's.

Matthew Hammond offered her his arm and escorted her to the dining room.

"You shall enjoy our winter, I think," he said.

"Oh?"

"There are skating parties. Ice skating. And in the evening, we go sledding."

"Really?" Mary glanced up. He did have a nice smile. His eyes were shining. He looked as if he wanted to laugh.

"One of the best hills is on Love Lane," he teased, laughing outright.

"That is a very bumpy road," a voice said. Mary turned around, startled. She had not realized Charles was right behind them.

Chapter 17

~~~~~~

It was after the train ride to New York that Mary realized she had lost control. No longer could she decide when to dream. One minute she would be in the present, and the next she would have slipped into the past.

She and Annie had been sitting in the streamlined metal car. Most of the train was filled with people on their way to do some Christmas shopping. Annie was talking with a woman across the aisle. Mary was looking out the large window, which was streaked and dirty.

Outside, steam had swirled around the train and enveloped them in a white, misty cloud. It blotted out the landscape beyond what had become a small window encased in wood, muffling the voices in the old car, which grew fainter and fainter. Mary rocked along in tune with the train, the seat beneath her soft, almost like velvet. But it was maroon plush, and she was sitting next to Julia, who was whispering to her. Mary could not hear her, for the whistle was blowing long and low, a mournful wail. Mary cried out.

"Mary!"

When she'd opened her eyes, Annie's hand was on her shoulder. The woman across the aisle was leaning over, peering at her. The man in front had craned his neck to stare.

"Are you all right, Mary?" Annie asked.

She managed to nod and then buried her face in Annie's shoulder.

"You cried out so pitifully!"

"A bad dream," Mary muttered.

She could hear Annie explaining, assuring the people around that Mary was all right. Mary felt distanced, as if she were wrapped in cotton.

Now it was Monday. Mary sat at her desk in school staring out the window. Ms. Martinez had given the class this period to work on their reports. A kaleidoscope of images tumbled in front of her, all she had to show for the weekend that had passed: The jingle of a horse's harness bells and a woolen blanket muffling her against the cold. She and Annie bouncing and tumbling in the back seat of a city cab. The taste of warm, spicy mince pie eaten from Charles's fork. Thin, gummy strings of cheese on the pizza Daddy had wanted her to eat. The clicking of the Pinkhams' phone as Julia had cranked the handle.

A chair scraped across the floor behind her. The playing fields out the window came back into focus. She turned to the paper on her desk—the half page she had written about Charles. She could not face Ms. Martinez.

When the bell rang, Mary was not expecting it. Class had seemed to last no more than five minutes. Papers rustled, books were dropped into bags, voices grew loud, someone laughed. Mary did not move. She sat, watching. If a student stopped to speak to Ms. Martinez, that would be her chance to escape.

"Hi, Mary Barrone."

She looked up at Mike. "Hi." Mary jumped to her feet. Maybe she could walk out with him, pretending to be deep in conversation.

"Mary." Ms. Martinez blocked the bottom of the aisle. "We have an appointment."

There was no choice but to follow her.

"See you later," Mike said.

Once they were seated in her office, Ms. Martinez asked to see Mary's work. Mary handed over the page. She stared at the floor. The rug was worn where the desk chair had rolled back and forth many times.

"Is this all of it?" the teacher asked.

Mary nodded, not looking up.

"Two short paragraphs that sound more like the beginning of a fairy tale than an English research paper?"

Mary licked her lips and continued to stare at the tracks in the rug.

164 ∽

"You must know this is unacceptable."

Mary knew she ought to be upset, but she felt as if this were happening to someone else.

"When we talked on Wednesday, you convinced me you were going to accomplish something over this weekend."

Mary swallowed and shrugged her shoulders.

She heard the teacher dialing the phone. "Pat?" Ms. Martinez said. "I have Mary Barrone in my office. She is failing English."

There was a silence.

"Really? I'm sorry to hear that, but I'm not surprised. Better get her parents in, right? Yes. Tomorrow if possible. Oh, and ask Carol Rosten to be at the meeting. Thanks, Pat."

Ms. Martinez hung up the phone. "I'm sure you realize I had to do that," she said. "Your guidance counselor is calling your parents. She just told me you are also failing French and social studies."

Mary stood up. "Can I go now?"

Ms. Martinez rose as well. She put her hand on Mary's shoulder. "I want to help you."

"I'm going to miss the late bus if I don't go." Mary pulled away. Ms. Martinez looked sad.

The house was empty when Mary arrived home. She went upstairs to her room. Out the window, the river was a pale silver ribbon in the distance. The sky was a fragile blue above the bare, brown trees.

Downstairs, the phone rang, shrill and insistent. She stayed motionless, stiff, waiting for it to stop. When it finally did, she let out her breath in a deep sigh. Maybe it had been her guidance counselor. Maybe she would give up for today. Maybe—

There was the sound of a car outside. Mary went over to the front window. Annie was getting out of the car. Brian was pulling bags of groceries from the back seat. Mary could see them talking, but could not hear what they were saying. Overwhelmed, Mary felt like crying.

The telephone rang again. Annie was just getting to the front steps. She might be too late to catch it. *Two. Three. Four. Five.* Annie and Brian were in the front hall. There was a muffled clatter as if something had dropped. *Six.*

Then it was still. Mary went back to her desk and sat in her chair. The book Mr. Gray had lent her was open to the picture of the station. She could disappear into it. Her stomach dropped sickeningly, and she jerked her head away.

"Mary!"

It was Annie calling. Mary did not answer.

Underneath the book, the corner of the *Science Today* article was visible. She almost laughed, thinking how innocent, how childish she had been. *To fly like Superman, to visit Einstein.* She had fallen through the rabbit hole of time.

The door from the second floor creaked. "Mary?" It was Annie.

Woodenly Mary got to her feet. "What?"

"You *are* here? I guess you didn't hear me from downstairs. You had a phone call."

"Who was it?"

"Mr. Gray from the Historical Society." Annie stood in the doorway. "He said he was expecting you this afternoon, but you didn't appear. I told him you are just so busy with schoolwork, it's a wonder you keep any appointments. I told him you would be sorry to have missed him. Was that all right?"

"Yes."

Mary had forgotten all about it. Mr. Gray had been looking for information about Charles so she could write her research paper. Maybe she should have told Ms. Martinez about that. These little hopeful thoughts kept trying to bubble to the surface, but, once there, they evaporated. It was too late.

Annie went on smiling and talking, smiling and talking.

A car screeched across the gravel below, its brakes squealing. Annie ran to the window as a door slammed. She turned to Mary, eyebrows raised, face serious. "It's your father," she said, moving quickly toward the stairs. "He's running like the house is on fire. Something terrible must have happened."

Something terrible. Mary began to tremble.

"*Mary!*" Her father's voice thundered up the stairs. "Come down here at once."

"What is it? What is it?" Annie called as she ran down.

Mary followed slowly. From the second floor she could see him standing in the front hall. His face looked gray, and a dark patch showed on one cheek.

"What's wrong, John?" Annie rushed up to him. Brian

came out of the living room, mouth open, staring at his stepfather.

"Go to your room, Brian. Mary, get down here!"

"What's going on?" Brian whispered as he brushed past her.

"In the living room." Her father jerked his thumb in that direction.

"Please, John," Annie begged. "Tell us what is the matter. You're frightening me."

"You'll see," he said, tight-lipped, steering Annie to the couch.

He pointed at a wing chair. "Sit down," he ordered Mary. He sat next to Annie, his lips clenched. He stared at Mary wordlessly for a long time. Not even Annie spoke.

"Well," he said finally, "I am at a loss."

"And so are we!" Annie was almost crying. "Please!"

"I had the strangest phone call of my life," he said. "In fact, I was sure it was some mistake. That's what I said to your guidance counselor, Mary. I said, 'You've got the wrong girl. My daughter's a straight-A student.' "

" 'Is this Mr. Barrone, B-A-R-R-O-N-E, father of Mary? You live at 1 Studwell Point?' the woman asked.

" 'Yes,' I said, 'but this is preposterous. My daughter studies all the time. She can't be failing.' "

"*Fail*-ing?"

"You're no more shocked than I was, Annie," he said.

"That's impossible." Annie's voice rose. "I've seen Mary poring over that book on Sound Port. And remember how excited she was about her report? This has to be a problem with the teacher."

"She's failing three subjects, not one. Could there be three teachers who just don't understand Mary?" His voice was harsh—a tone he had never used with Mary. "How could you lie to us?"

"Lie?" Mary had not thought she was lying.

"I don't know what else you'd call it," her father said. "All this homework you were doing? Day and night! Even Thanksgiving Day, you had homework to do! Homework came before everything else. It certainly came before your family."

"John," Annie said. "Don't."

"Annie, we've been betrayed. We've been had. I can't get over it. When I think how often I asked my child— no, I practically begged her for a little bit of her time...."

"I'm sorry," Mary said.

"Sorry? I guess you're sorry." Her father brought his fist down on the coffee table in front of him. "Just what were you doing when you were supposed to be studying? Tell me that!"

Mary looked up at him.

"Dreaming," she said.

"Dreaming? What kind of an answer is that?"

"John, stop yelling at the child. What do you expect her to say when you holler at her like that?" Annie came over and knelt down by Mary's chair. "Sweetheart, we know you didn't fail on purpose. You wouldn't do that. I think you've got something—like mono, maybe. You haven't had any appetite for weeks, and you look tired all the time."

"There could be another reason for that. I never thought I'd be asking you such a question." He shook his head in disbelief. "Mary, are you taking drugs?"

"*Drugs!*" Mary was shocked. "I'd never do that!"

"Of course she wouldn't, John. That's a terrible thing to say." Annie stroked Mary's hand. "Your dad didn't mean that. Tell her you didn't mean it, John."

"I don't know what to think. But I'm going to get to the bottom of this! Now, Mary, I want some answers. We're meeting with your teachers, the social worker, and your guidance counselor at eight o'clock in the morning. What are we supposed to say to them?"

Mary shrugged.

"Look at me when I'm talking to you," her father said.

Mary looked at him. A vein stood out in his forehead.

"We'll tell them Mary must be ill," Annie answered for her.

"Mary? Do you have any explanation?"

She shook her head.

"I'm waiting, Mary. I'm waiting for you to tell me what's going on. Annie's suggested that you're sick or that your teachers don't understand you. What do you suggest?"

She had told him the truth. He wouldn't listen. "I don't know," she said.

"You know what I want you to do? I want you to go to your room. Get out your notebooks in French, English, and social studies, and bring them here. We have to start somewhere."

Mary got up and walked out of the living room. At the bottom of the stairs, she looked back. Her father seemed to have sagged. He was slumped down on the sofa, his head in his hands.

" 'Bye, Daddy," she whispered, and ran up the stairs.

Chapter 18

~~~~~~

Lying on some sort of hard board, Mary was sway-
ing dizzily from side to side. Strong arms circled her
from the back. Legs were braced against hers, keeping
her from flying away as she was hurtled through space.
She was pulled to the left, leaning hard, fighting a force
that would propel her to the right. Somewhere a siren
wailed.

She forced her eyes open, squinting in the onrushing air.
Someone was screaming, screaming in fear or exhilaration,
a scream she might hear in an amusement park.
"It's all right! I've got you!" It was Charles, shouting
over the wind. "We're almost out of the turn! There!"
Ahead, Mary could see a snow-covered road, sloping
down a long hill. The board beneath her had become a

172 ⌇

sled, and it slowed slightly as they straightened out. She took a deep breath, and the screaming stopped.

"We did it! Bravo!" Charles exulted. Below them, dark shapes appeared in the light of a bonfire. As Mary relaxed against Charles, there was a crunch beneath their runners.

The sled left the ground, twisted violently, and knocked Mary into the air. She plunged head first, arms flying, into the cold white embrace of a snowbank.

There was a muffled sound—like short blasts on a foghorn. Or an ambulance. Hands grasped her under the arms and pulled backward. Her head flopped about. There was a voice—but it was far away—like a radio with the volume set too low. Mary cried out but made no sound. More hands gripped her ankles, her arms, her shoulders. She tried to protest.

"Be careful with her!"

Daddy? No, it couldn't be.

"Steady there."

"Is she all right?"

"She's just had the wind knocked out of her."

"Can you stand up, Christabel?"

Mary became aware of the crowd around her. Charles was supporting her, brushing snow from her head. Julia was glaring.

"Charles, you were going much too fast!"

"Not now, Julia!" Mary was picked up and carried down the hill, then tucked into a carriage. "We'll get her home safe and sound."

"Put her down, Charles!"

"She's light as a feather. No trouble at all. I'll just carry her up to her room, and you can tuck her in."

And she and Julia were in a bedroom, and the minutes or hours in between had disappeared or never been.

Full white curtains enclosed an alcove containing a built-in bed. On the fireplace mantel, the pendulum of a clock clicked as it swung back and forth, loud in the silence.

Mary was wearing a white nightgown, high at the neck, that cascaded to the floor. Julia pulled back the bed curtains and turned down a coverlet. Mary lifted the gown with both hands to climb the steps which led to the high bed.

"I'll send Maude with some hot tea. You don't seem to be injured," Julia said brusquely.

Mary snuggled down in a lacy cocoon. She was shaken by chills that made her teeth chatter. It was some time later that the curtain moved, and a cool hand touched her forehead. "Are you awake, dear girl?" Charles asked.

"We'll take care of Christabel, Charles!" A gas lamp on the wall illuminated Julia standing in the doorway. Next to her, Maude carried a cup on a tray.

Charles drew back abruptly, then leaned down and kissed Mary's brow. "Very good, Julia," he said, moving away from the bed.

The women came closer. Their shadows preceded them in the lamplight and fell across Mary, veiling her in darkness.

Time was elastic. Sometimes the clock would clang

174 ✆

*away the hours in rapid succession, the pendulum a blur
as it swung from side to side. Or it would slow down, and
Mary would experience some events in a three-quarters
tempo, where the hands on the clock seemed to melt and
ooze like a Dali painting.*

*Places blurred, ran into one another. Thinking she was
listening to the clock in her bedroom, she looked up and
saw the grandfather clock in the drawing room. Mary
became aware of voices coming from the library, raised in
anger.*

*"You are not the same person since Christabel arrived!"
It was Julia speaking.*

*"I don't know what you mean," Charles answered. "I
have been kind to the girl for your sake. She is your niece."*

"Rather more than kind."

"Your insinuations, Julia, are insulting."

*"Your behavior, Charles, is exasperating. You are ne-
glecting your work. You barely go to your study. You are
constantly planning amusements for her. To speak frankly,
you are acting her age, not your own!"*

*"And you are acting the jealous matron. Hardly becom-
ing, my dear."*

*Jealous! Mary felt she must have misheard. That could
not be possible. Beautiful Julia jealous of her?*

"Why don't you go home?" a voice hissed.

*Mary's hand flew to her throat. She turned. Maude
stood behind her, face dark, eyes glaring. "Witch!" she
said in Mary's ear.*

*Witch. Witch. Witch. The hated word reverberated,
bouncing off the walls. Witch. Witch. Witch.*

Mary wrung her hands. Somewhere a doorbell chimed.

And she was twisting a velvet cushion. It was soft under her fingertips. She was sitting in the bay window of the parlor. She looked down at her dress. It was a deep wine color, made from a shiny material that shimmered with the waves in the texture.

Maude was gone. Julia sat across from her, staring.

Footsteps crossed the uncarpeted front hall, and soon Maude appeared in the doorway. Mary winced. The woman did not look at her. "Mr. Matthew Hammond," she announced.

Matthew Hammond came in. He bowed first to Julia, then to Mary. "Good afternoon, ladies. I hope you are quite recovered, Miss Kirkland?"

"Recovered?"

"I understand you had a sledding mishap last week."

"Last week?"

"Christabel, you sound like an echo. It was not major," Julia told Matthew. "Fortunately, Christabel was not injured. Do sit down, Matthew. Here is Maude with the tea."

Maude put a large silver tray on the table next to Julia. Charles appeared as Julia was pouring the tea.

"This is unexpected," Julia said.

"The writing is not going smoothly today." Charles came in and took a seat between Mary and Matthew. "I thought a diversion might help. And how are you, Matthew?" he asked. "Did your shooting expedition go well?"

"We bagged quite a few grouse." Matthew smiled, obviously pleased.

176 ∾

Mary made a face.

"Is something wrong, Miss Kirkland?" Matthew asked.

"I just don't believe in shooting birds or animals," Mary said.

"But surely you hunt in the West?" Matthew looked puzzled. "It's rather a necessity of life."

They were all looking at Mary strangely. They did not understand her twentieth-century viewpoint, Mary realized. She tried to think of something to say; then Charles came to her rescue.

"Such a tender little heart," he said. "We shall certainly not let you see fresh game."

"Christabel is hardly that delicate, Charles." Julia frowned, then changed the subject. "Have you heard? The Edison Company is installing an electric generator. They will be able to pull a switch and have lamps lit the length of Main Street. It's hard to imagine."

Lights lit the length of Main Street. Mary thought about downtown Sound Port. Soon there would be Christmas lights on all the store fronts. They were probably up by now. And the wreaths on every lamppost . . .

". . . bunch of outsiders bringing in electricity," Matthew was saying. "Father says it will be double the cost of kerosene."

"I'll have this house wired," Charles said. "Have to keep pace, or you'll be left in the dark."

"Hmmph!" Matthew looked annoyed, and Julia gave Charles a disapproving look.

"We'll have your father over and show him the advantages. Has he given in on the telephone, by the way?"

"By no means." Matthew shook his head. "Father feels it is an instrument designed to invade one's privacy. However, we do have a telephone at the firehouse. I believe it may save people's homes."

"You are a part of the new volunteer fire department?" Charles asked.

Matthew nodded.

"What equipment do you have?"

Mary pictured the firehouse in Sound Port. The largest building in their small town, its clock could be seen the length of Main Street. She could almost hear its whistle blowing for school closings on snow days. She felt odd suddenly. There was a hollow feeling in her stomach, as if she were hungry. But it was not food that she craved.

". . . just one hand-drawn pumper." Matthew was speaking.

"In that case, one hopes the fires are confined to the vicinity of the fire station." Charles laughed. "Otherwise you fellows won't get to them in time to be any use."

"We do our best, sir." Matthew sat up, rigid.

Mary bit her lip. There were such undercurrents in the room. Mary was not immune. She could almost see HA-TRED spelled out in the air when Maude looked at her. Her heart beat at the thought, thumping in her chest.

Beep! Beep! Beep! Beep! The noise pulsated, sounded insistently. Then the beeps merged into one long alarm. Feet pounded across the floor, coming closer. Loud words were spoken but had no meaning. An object covered her mouth, and she struggled to free herself.

"Christabel!"

Mary blinked and looked at Julia, who was standing in front of the fireplace. Mary was lying on the divan, covered with an afghan. Charles and Matthew were gone. Julia crossed over to her and picked up a book that had evidently fallen to the floor. She held it out to Mary. "How much of the poem have you memorized?"

Mary sat up and rubbed her eyes. She squinted, looking at the verse.

> *"With open eyes (ah woe is me!)*
> *Asleep, and dreaming—"*

She stopped and stared at the final word.

" 'Asleep, and dreaming fearfully.' " Julia finished the line. "Why do you look so frightened?" she asked.

"Who? Who—is having—fearful dreams?"

"Christabel, of course. In the poem she is under a spell." Julia looked at Mary and smiled, but there was no warmth in it. "Do not be concerned. You are much more likely to be the one who bewitches rather than the one who is bewitched."

"Julia!" Mary was close to tears. "What have I done? Are you mad at me?"

"Mad? That's a strange expression. I am certainly not mad. A trifle piqued, perhaps. Oh, don't look so stricken." She moved to the door. "Come along. I have a painting I want to show you. It's drying in the summerhouse."

They were taking cloaks from a closet beneath the staircase when Charles came down the stairs. He kissed Julia on the cheek, then took Mary's elbow. "I would like a private word with Christabel," he said.

"Really, Charles? More secrets?" Julia frowned.

"Just Christmas talk, my dear," he said, "which you must not be privy to. Come along upstairs for a moment, Christabel."

Charles led the way to the tower room. The words from the poem went round and round in Mary's mind. "Ah woe is me! Ah woe is me!" Charles had not let go of her hand, and he intertwined his fingers with hers as they went up the little stairway to his room. "Asleep, and dreaming . . . fearfully."

The sun was shining through the windows. Like Julia's smile, it gave no warmth. Charles seemed to read her thoughts. "It is a cold winter sun," he said, "so distant from the earth. We approach that solstice where darkness dominates." He brought her hand to his lips and kissed her fingers. "But, you, child of spring, will bring us light."

Involuntarily, Mary jerked her hand away.

Charles face reddened, and he walked behind his desk. He opened a drawer and took out a rectangular black velvet box. He held it out to Mary. "It's Julia's Christmas present. Do you think she will like it?"

Mary opened the box. Inside was a gold watch on a long chain, its round face encircled with diamonds.

"Try it on," Charles said. "I want to see that it looks right on a beautiful woman."

Mary picked up the watch. There was an inscription on the back which said "J.C.P. to J.E.P. Christmas, 1893."

"Eighteen ninety-three?"

Charles lifted his eyebrows, puzzled. "That is the year."

Mary tried to remember what Mr. Gray had said. 1897. The house had been sold by a person named Holden in 1897.

"Do put it on," Charles urged, coming from behind the desk. He took the chain from her and fastened the watch around her neck, then turned her to face him. "Ah, lovely," he said. She looked down at the watch, still trying to sort out her thoughts. In a little over four years Charles and Julia would no longer be here. Why?

"You don't seem to like it much," Charles said. "You are saying nothing."

"I do like it. It is very beautiful, like Julia."

Stepping back, she slipped the watch over her head. She replaced it in the velvet box.

"Father Christmas has a few other surprises up his sleeve." Charles smiled at her and put the box in his desk. "I'm at a crucial point in my play. I hope to have the first draft done by Christmas."

"I'd like to read it," Mary said.

"Actually, you might be able to help me. This morning I'm having real difficulty with one scene. You remember I was looking for the person or event that showed the main character how shallow his life had become?"

Mary nodded.

"Well, I've found it. He has fallen in love with his wife's younger sister. It has taken me completely by surprise. Characters have a way of dictating to their creators. So I'm in a quandary. I have this older man hopelessly in love with a girl twenty years his junior."

Charles paused. Mary said nothing.

"It's her reaction that I can't work out," Charles resumed. "How does this enchanting young creature react to her much older relative? Would she be frightened? Angry perhaps?" He came back around and leaned against the desk, looking into Mary's eyes. "Is it possible she could love him—"

"Miss Christabel!"

Mary and Charles both jumped.

"Why are you creeping about, Maude? You might knock," Charles said angrily.

"The doors were open, sir," Maude replied. "And the missus sent me to fetch her niece." She eyed Mary coldly.

"Ah, well," Charles said more quietly. "I will have to hear your opinion of my play another time, Christabel. Run along to Julia, then."

There was a very bright light, making it impossible for Mary to open her eyes. She tried to move her head, but it was as if she were held in a vise. She heard people whispering, bodiless voices. The light went in circles, making patterns on her closed lids.

Outside the window, Mary could see snow falling, the flakes pinging on the panes, then melting. The snowflakes swirled and whirled, and the music of the Christmas ball swelled and ebbed in the rhythms of a waltz.

Greens hung in swags over mantels and doors, and their piney smell mingled with the scents of spices in the steaming wassail bowl.

"What is today?" Mary asked breathlessly. "What is the date?"

"The tenth of December," her partner, a mustached young man, answered.

"I'd like to sit down, please," Mary said.

"Certainly." As they walked across the floor, there was a flourish, and the music stopped. The young man escorted her to the side of the room where chairs were lined up.

The tenth of December. Mary was unable to add up the days since she had left home. But there must have been many. The tenth of December.

Someone was bending over her. She looked up at Matthew Hammond. "I have the next dance, I believe," he said, offering his arm. He steered her to the far end of the room, where they stood apart, waiting for the music.

"You look particularly beautiful tonight, Miss Kirkland," Matthew said.

The music began, and he put his hand on her waist. "And now I have an excuse to hold you. Though I wish it were not at arm's length."

They glided across the polished floor, twirling and dipping in the outer circle of dancers. Bright candles flickered on the Christmas tree, handsome women in silks and velvets smiled at dark-suited men, and there was the swish of skirts, whispering beneath the music.

Outside, the snow continued to fall. Mary danced with another partner, then another. Men bowed and she curtseyed and they danced, and it all blended together. She went round and round, round and round, until she was light-headed from the dizzying circles.

Somehow she managed to get to the back door. She pressed her face against the glass. The white falling snow made the back yard bright. "Will you come back with me when it snows, Mary Barrone?" *Mike's voice was so clear in her mind, she turned to see if he was beside her. She had not forgotten her promise. It had been with her all evening, ever since the snow had started to fall.*

It was a promise she would never keep.

But she could go to the holly grove. She was drawn to the outside. Quietly she slipped out the door and across the back yard. The snow was falling thickly, making it difficult for her to see as it gathered on her lashes. She stopped at the edge of the woods. If she went down the path, the snow would engulf her, surround her, and she might disappear.

She turned around. On her left a faint light gleamed. It was coming from the summerhouse. The building was ghostlike in the white flakes that fell like a silent curtain around it.

Mary shivered, wondering if some other soul had been drawn away from the warmth of the ball to the cold beauty of the snow-filled night.

Mary crossed the white lawn and went inside the summerhouse.

Oil lamps glowed on either side of a fireplace. She walked over to the fire and held out her cold hands. Waves of warmth melted the snow on her dress.

An easel was set up, and on it was a charcoal drawing. A sketch that Julia was doing of Christabel was nearly

184 ✂

finished. As she leaned over to examine it, Mary was startled by a voice behind her.

"Are you exhausted, dear child? I saw you go outside and followed you. I was worried about you," Charles said.

He kissed the top of her head. "You are bare-headed and coatless. You must be careful not to catch a chill." He stroked her arms, then took her hands in his. "You are ice-cold, little one." He crossed her arms in front of her, holding her close.

Mary could not move.

He put his chin on her shoulder, his head touching hers. "That picture does not do you justice. It has no color. It cannot show your eyes, as green as the sea at Capri. Nor your hair, like sunshine on a wheat field. And where is the skin aglow with the passion of youth . . ."

He should not be talking to her like this, Mary knew, and yet she remained motionless.

" 'It was a lovely sight to see / The lady Christabel . . .' " She felt his lips brush her cheek.

"No," Mary whispered.

"What am I doing? What am I doing?" Charles turned her toward him. She caught a glimpse of a face in the window. Charles's mouth was drawn back in anguish. "God help me."

He kissed her—her closed eyes, her cheeks, and then her mouth. She pulled back desperately, but stayed in his embrace. Charles was crying. "I love you," he said over and over. "I love you. I'm sorry."

"The window!" Mary cried, but he did not understand.

He lifted her chin. "Look at me, my darling. Say you love me. At least that, for the misery I'm going to cause."

"Charles!"

Julia stood in the doorway.

Mary began to shake. She tried to pull away from Charles, but he gripped her shoulder and held her against him.

"You've lost your mind!" Julia cried.

"I have, Julia. I have. Over her." His face contorted, in pain.

"You can't mean this!"

"I do. I love her, and I'm sorry. I would never want to hurt you, Julia."

Mary pulled his hand from her shoulder and broke away. "Stop it. Please! Stop it!"

Julia had started to cry. "You!" She sobbed. "You—Maude warned me about you."

"It's not her fault. I'm a foolish man."

Julia snatched the sketch from the easel. Holding it in front of Mary, she ripped it in half and then ripped it in two again. "That's what I think of you."

"Julia, don't!" Charles went to her and grabbed her arms, pulling her away. "It's enough that one of us is mad."

"Go pack your trunk!" Julia turned on Mary. "You are leaving in the morning."

"No. I'm leaving tonight," Charles said.

"Charles! No!" Julia threw her arms around him. "Please! She'll go away. I'm sending her away!" She collapsed against him, weeping.

"Julia, you will break my heart. I have to leave. I cannot stay here after what has happened."

"It is my heart that will break." Julia's words were muffled.

There was a terrible lump in Mary's throat. She tried to swallow. Charles was looking at her over Julia's head. His eyes pleaded with her.

"Come back! Come back! Come back!" The voice begged.

It must be Charles.

"I miss you. I love you. Can you hear me, Mary?"

But I don't love you. You've ruined everything.

"Mary! Mary! Mary!" The crying had grown louder. "I'll never call you contrary again."

Mary? Mary? Mary? Not Christabel?

"Her eyes fluttered, Ma! Watch! I saw her lids move. Mary! Open your eyes!"

"Mary, come back to us!" It was another voice.

"Daddy . . ."

"Thank God! Thank God!"

Chapter 19

"What's a coma like, huh? What does it feel like?" Brian was sitting in a chair next to Mary's bed, swinging his legs.

Mary's arm was sore where the I.V. needle dripped fluid into her vein. She moved, but that only made it worse, and she settled back. "What's a coma like?" Mary echoed.

"Yeah. That's what you had. You looked like you were asleep, but we couldn't wake you up." Brian brought his face close to Mary's. "I was scared. We kept calling you. Couldn't you hear us?"

"No. At least, I don't think so. A coma's like a lot of blankness sometimes—and—and—other stuff."

"You remember waking up last night?" Brian asked.

"Kind of," Mary said. She was struggling to sort out hazy impressions.

"It was late. Ma was about to take me home, and I saw you were moving, kind of jerking around, you know? You'd done that before, but I said to Dad, 'Let me try. Let me try.' And I started calling your name, and I called it, and I called it—" Brian was running out of breath. "And you opened your eyes."

Something had happened. Something was wrong. Mary fought to remember.

"You cried. Ma said it was because you were so glad to wake up. You cried a lot. Then you went back to sleep. Ma and Dad took turns staying here all night."

Mary had been drifting in and out of sleep. She remembered opening her eyes during the night. The room had been dark except for a garish light that came from behind her. It illuminated the bedcovers and her father sitting in a chair next to her. He was holding her hand. Then she had fallen asleep again and awakened in the gray light of early morning with a sense of loss. That was what nagged at her now.

"What are you staring at, huh? You look funny. Are you okay?" Brian jumped out of his chair and started for the door. "I'll get the nurse."

"No. Don't, Brian. I'm all right. I'm just trying to remember . . ."

"What happened? That what you want to know?"

"Yes," Mary said.

"You and your father had a fight. You went to your

room. I was upstairs. I could hear Ma arguing with him in the living room. After a while, he came up. He knocked on your door, and you didn't answer. He said, 'Mary, come down here right now.' I'd never heard Sir John yell like that. Then he ran up the little stairs to your room. He started hollering for Ma to call 911. The ambulance came—lights flashing and everything. Nobody could wake you up. They brought you here."

Brian was talking fast. Mary's head was spinning. She had to hold on, or she'd . . . she'd weave her crazy circles to the past. The memory of the summerhouse flooded over her, and her lips began to tremble. "No!" she said aloud.

Brian's face loomed close to hers. "I wasn't supposed to talk about it. I forgot. Don't cry. Please. Don't cry."

"Brian!" she said, willing herself to stay in the room, to see him.

"I shouldn't have told you." Brian's voice dropped to a whisper. "But I need to know about it. See? It could happen to me, too. There's a lady—they thought her husband gave her insulin, or maybe she took it herself— she's been in a coma for years."

"Oh, Brian," Mary said. She could see how frightened he was. She wished she could think straight, enough to comfort him.

"I'm afraid someday I'll go to sleep and never wake up."

"That's not going to happen." Mary's tears were now for Brian. "Honest. Look. I woke up." She sniffled and swallowed hard. "Brian, we'll talk about this. When I'm feeling better. Okay?"

"Yeah. 'Cause you understand, Mary." He was looking at the I.V. in her arm.

Mary remembered how the needle and cotton in their bathroom had disgusted her. It made her ashamed. "Yes, I do," she said. "I understand."

"Good morning!" A dark-haired nurse came into the room. "You're awake again. Wonderful!" She tousled Brian's hair. "You wait outside. I'm going to give your sister a wash."

Brian got slowly to his feet.

"I won't be long. I promise." The nurse gave him a gentle pat, sending him in the direction of the door. "Scoot now."

He turned back to Mary.

"I'll go get Ma and Dad. They're having coffee. I was supposed to tell them when you woke up."

The nurse closed the door behind him. "That child has been practically glued to your bedside," she told Mary. She raised the bed until Mary was almost sitting up, then brought a basin of warm water, soap, and a washcloth from the bathroom. After washing Mary, she said, "Okay, sleeping beauty, let's see what we can do with your hair."

Mary put her hand to her head. Her hair felt limp and greasy.

"Maybe tomorrow you'll be able to have a shower and shampoo," the nurse said, as she combed Mary's hair.

"I'm going to bring you some gelatin and broth. The sooner you eat, the sooner we can disconnect the I.V. and get you out of here." She took the basin off the table and raised the top. Inside the lid a mirror was attached. "Want to get reacquainted?" The nurse tipped the mirror so Mary could see herself.

For the flick of a second, Mary saw Christabel looking back at her, thick ash-blond curls framing her face, tears running down her cheeks. Mary squeezed her eyes shut, and when she opened them, her own image appeared. Her face was white and thin. There were circles under her eyes, and her lank hair hung, lifeless and dull. She looked away.

"What day is it?"

"Sunday," the nurse replied.

"The date, I mean."

"December eleventh." She walked over and opened the door. "You can come back in now, little brother."

"They were already here!" Brian announced.

Mary's father and Annie rushed into the room and to either side of the bed, bumping heads as they leaned down to kiss her.

"Ow!" Annie straightened up. "Wouldn't it be just our luck to knock each other out!"

Her father's eyes were wet as he bent back down to kiss her cheek. "Sweetheart . . ."

"I'm sorry, Daddy."

"Sorry! You have nothing to be sorry about," Annie said. "It was a virus, but it's over. The nightmare is over."

"A few days' rest, and the doctor says you can come home," her father said.

"Mary's coming home! Mary's coming home!" Brian jumped up and down at the foot of her bed.

"Hush, Briny. Mary's still weak. We don't want to wear her out."

"You have to eat, get your strength back," her father said.

"We'll have you all better before Christmas," Annie said.

"A virus?" Mary was trying to piece it together.

"That's all they can come up with," her father said. "Except anemia."

"No wonder you're anemic," Annie said. "Every time we turned around they were taking more blood for tests. Scared us to death. Tested for encephalitis, tuberculosis, meningitis—"

"The point is," her father interrupted, "nothing showed up, thank God, so they are assuming a viral infection."

"You must have been fighting it for months," Annie said. "No wonder you had trouble in school. I've talked to all your teachers, by the way, and—"

"Not now, Annie. Mary's looking tired. As you said, we don't want to wear her out."

"Breakfast." The dark-haired nurse came in with a tray, which she put down on Mary's table and then positioned the table over her lap.

"I'll help you, Sam," her father said when she made no

move to pick up the spoon. He held it to her lips, and she sipped the broth.

"Come on, Bri. We'll go have a snack in the cafeteria," Annie said.

Mary felt like a little girl as her father fed her. It was a good feeling.

She ate everything on the tray. Her father moved the table away and lowered her bed. "You take it easy, now. We'll go home and come back this afternoon. Okay?"

"Thanks, Daddy."

He started to turn away, but hesitated, and turned back. He looked down at her. "I thought we were going to lose you," he said. "Day after day, I sat here, knowing you were gone somewhere far out of reach. It was the loneliest feeling. Like falling into a black hole." He kissed her forehead. "Sam," he said, his voice almost a whisper. "I'm sorry. I'm so sorry for getting angry with you. I should have known you were sick. . . ."

"Daddy, don't!" Mary cried, almost in tears. "Don't blame yourself. I can't bear it. Please!"

"*Shh, shh,* sweetheart." He smoothed her hair. "I won't say any more if it upsets you. Anyway, you're back. That's all that matters." He walked to the door. "See you later, sweetheart."

Back. Yes, Mary knew she was back. But she was precarious. She felt as if she were walking on thin gauze, and that if she was not careful, she might fall through and end up in that other time. Charles and Julia. It hurt her to think about them. They had been so beautiful, so perfect until . . . She pushed the thought away. It was over. She would never return.

Information trickled to Mary over the next few days. Her parents and the school were blaming the unnamed virus for Mary's failure. She would be given time to make up her work. If she were not strong enough, she could complete the semester in summer school.

There were get-well cards from her English teacher and her guidance counselor. There was a book from Mr. Gray. Annie had filled the room with flowers.

On Tuesday afternoon, there was a knock, and Mike Bell stuck his head through the partially opened door. "You up to company, Mary Barrone?"

"Oh." Mary was taken by surprise. Her hand flew to her hair. Thank goodness, she had been able to shampoo it. It felt soft and clean. "I thought you were my folks."

"Okay if I come in?"

"Yes. Sure. Come in."

Mike walked over to the bed and handed her a large poster. There were drawings and messages. "From the kids in English class," Mike said.

"This is so nice!" Mary looked at the top of the enormous card. GET WELL! WE MISS YOU! it said. Many of the drawings were taken from *The Odyssey*. Calypso's island and the land of the lotus eaters were among them. On the island labeled "Ithaca," someone had put a photograph of the school.

"The message is," Mike explained, "you've been veg-ging out in the hospital long enough. It's time you came back to the real world."

"Where's yours?" Mary looked again at the poster.

"You ought to be able to find it," Mike teased. "If you remember a walk we took."

And there it was, a sprig of live holly fastened to the bottom of the card. It glistened, and when Mary looked closer, she saw it had been dusted with glittery white powder. "Snow?" she asked.

"Uh-huh," Mike said. "It snowed one evening while you were sick. I came to the hospital that night and then I went out to the holly grove. I had some dumb idea I'd find you there. Not exactly find you in person, you know. But we had that deal—to be there together when it snowed. I just had to go. Sound nuts?"

"Oh, no," Mary said. "Not at all." She hesitated a moment. Mike had taken a risk, telling her that. She could be brave, too. "I think I dreamed about you."

"In the holly grove?"

"No. I was in—my house. It was snowing outside. I could see the snow melting on the windowpanes. It was December the tenth. I even remember the date. I started to go to the holly grove, but—I never made it."

"I would have been there." Mike's face flushed. "Spooky stuff, huh? You think we have ESP or something?"

"Sounds like it," Mary said.

"Anyway, the next time it snows, if you're out of here, we'll go to the holly grove together. For real." Mike took the poster from her and propped it up on a windowsill. Then he came back and encircled her wrist with two fingers. "You've gotten awful skinny," he said.

"Well, hell-*oo!*" Annie burst into the room. "Uh-oh," she said, "I hope we're not interrupting. Look who's here, John." She half turned to Mary's father behind her. "It's Michael. We're so glad to see you." Annie waved at Mike, who had let go Mary's wrist.

"I just brought Mary something the gang in school made." Mike pointed at the card.

Mary wondered why she wasn't embarrassed. Annie's voice was full of innuendo as she commented on Mike's many visits. She went on and on about how faithful he had been, how encouraging, what a comfort to the family. Mike looked a little uncomfortable, but he had an easy way about him of laughing it off, and he didn't leave. Then he told a funny story about Christmas shopping and had them all laughing. The laughter encircled Mary's bed and closed her in its warmth.

"You're starting to look like yourself again, Sam," her father said and beamed.

"I think I am myself again," Mary said.

Chapter 20

It was a week before the doctor found Mary well enough to leave the hospital. By then she had begun to gain a little weight, and her blood tests showed a decrease in the anemia. Since it was only a few days until Christmas recess, Mary did not attend classes. She was sent work to make up at home, and it was agreed she would return to school after the holidays.

Coming home in that season was magical. When they'd first moved in, Mary had barely noticed the beautifully shaped spruces on either side of the front door. Now they were adorned with white lights, and the oval panes of glass in the door were edged by evergreens, also strung with lights.

The front hall had been completely redone. Annie had been afraid Mary would be disappointed because

198 ⌒

she had been unable to find anything like the old paper. She had settled for something much lighter. Mary was relieved. She wanted no reminders of the house as it had been.

Garlands of green roping decorated the banister leading to the second floor, and a large red bow hung from the newel post. There was a new mirror on the wall, and a matching velvet bow was attached to the top. Mistletoe hung from the chandelier in the middle of the hall.

A fire burned in the living room fireplace, and a tree stood ready to decorate in front of the bay window. Annie had, as her father said, "worked her butt off" for Mary's homecoming. She had bought old glass ornaments in antique shops and had popcorn and cranberries ready to string. It was old-fashioned and wonderful; homey rather than elegant. It suited Mary fine.

She entered into the Christmas festivities, grateful for her family's love. She went shopping with Annie, slipping away to buy her stepmother a Christmas T-shirt with a star that lit up. Annie was so pleased she wore it almost daily through the holidays.

But sometimes, outside the stores, Salvation Army Santas rang their bells, and they would echo for Mary with the sound of sleigh bells. In the window of a brightly lit jewelry shop, a bejeweled watch shone against black velvet. Then Mary would wonder: Did Charles leave? Had he given Julia the watch? Had she, Mary, messed up their lives? She would not go back to find out. She would never go back.

She continued to absorb herself in Christmas. She and

Brian decorated eggs with sequins and ribbons. She helped Annie bake cookies. Fragments of memories would be set off by the smell of gingerbread or the scent of cinnamon. Or, walking up the stairs to her tower, she would catch a glimpse of Charles on the stairs above her, or hear Julia's laughter. Mary's heart would beat fast, pounding loudly in her ears, and she would have to stop what she was doing and wait for the moment to pass.

At night, when she lay in her bed, she would say over and over, "I will not fly. I will not fly. I will never fly again." In the morning she would wake, grateful to find herself still in her room. And so she anchored herself in the present.

Christmas morning, Brian woke her as it was getting light, and they crept down to the living room. Presents were piled high under the tree. They turned on the tree lights and took their stockings down from the mantel. It was the first time Mary had hung her stocking since she left Freedom. She felt like a kid again, sitting on the floor with Brian, dumping out their stockings. "I'll bet there's an orange in the toe," Brian said.

"There's always an orange in the toe." Mary pulled hers out and held it up. "It wouldn't be Christmas without it."

There were also earrings and fancy face creams, a velvet hair bow, and multicolored hair ribbons in Mary's stocking. It was obvious Annie had done the shopping; yet nothing was outlandish, as Mary might have expected. Annie had chosen carefully to please Mary.

"Hey, look at this!" Brian held up a set of X-Acto

knives. "I'll be able to make all kinds of stuff with these."

"Do you like them? Santa do all right?" Mary's father and Annie, in bathrobes, stood in the doorway.

"They're neat!" Brian jumped up.

"Well, if you're going to work with small objects, you need the right tools," his stepfather said.

"You picked them out?" Brian looked surprised.

John Barrone nodded.

"Hey, thanks, Dad."

The grownups had hung stockings as well. Everyone laughed when Mary's father found a half-banana in the toe of his stocking. Annie liked to kid him about eating only half a banana on his cereal and leaving the other half in the fruit bowl.

It was a wonderful Christmas. Annie glowed with joy, and her happiness was contagious. She had researched Italian customs and prepared an Italian Christmas feast. She said if their name was Barrone, they ought to eat like Barrones.

Mary's father gave a blessing before the meal. "We are thankful for our new family, which has been guided through difficult times and emerged stronger. We are especially thankful for our beloved daughter, who was returned to our midst, and who brings joy to this glorious day."

"Amen," they all said.

Mary found herself looking at her stepmother a lot that Christmas Day. She was not like Mary's mother, and she was not like beautiful Julia, but she was all right. A little loud, a little kooky, but herself. She tried.

Mary tried, too. Annie wanted the house as finished as possible for the party the next weekend. In the days after Christmas, Mary helped her put the last touches on the dining room. They washed windows and hung drapes.

For the most part, Mary was able to keep the past out of her mind. It was, then, a little unsettling to receive on Thursday a reply from Metropolitan State College. She felt as if she had written to them in another lifetime.

The large thick envelope contained a letter thanking her for her interest and asking her to participate in dream experiments. Never! she thought to herself. The case studies she had requested were included. She decided to read them, but found no relationship to her own experience. Then she pictured how she might have been described. *Mary B., a fifteen-year-old subject . . .*

"Mary." Annie came into the kitchen where she was sitting. "Look who's here."

Mary winced. Mike had walked in behind her stepmother. She wished Annie wouldn't smirk and act so pleased whenever he showed up.

"You and Brian want to go ice-skating?" Mike asked.

"Brian's at a friend's," Mary said. "And I haven't been on skates for over two years."

"But you got new skates for Christmas. It's a good chance to try them out," Annie said.

"It's like riding a bike. You never forget." Mike held out his hand. "Come on. There's a swell pond right in the nature preserve."

Mary had been listening daily to the weather report.

Though she did not admit it to herself, she was hoping snow would be forecast. Not a flake had fallen. It had been dry and cold, with the temperature in the teens.

She let Mike pull her to her feet. She had grown up next to a creek in Freedom and had skated there all her life. She should do all right.

They drove back to the main gates of the nature preserve, and Mike parked his Jeep next to the old house that had been turned into park headquarters. Less than half a mile down an unmarked trail, they came to the pond.

"I never knew this was here," Mary said, looking out over the ice. The pond was the size of a couple of football fields and formed two uneven ovals with a narrow passage in the middle. At the far end, four teen-aged boys were playing hockey. Otherwise, the pond was empty.

"Not many people have found this," Mike said. "I'm sharing with you all the secrets of the woods."

Not quite all, Mary thought, and wished she could tell him her secrets.

They sat on benches in a wooden shelter and put on their skates. The ice was black and smooth, and their blades made the first lines in its surface.

Mary felt a little shaky at first, but Mike held her arm. They circled the pond twice, and she could almost feel her ankles getting stronger, her feet surer. The rhythmic push and glide became automatic and exhilarating.

Mike was a good skater, though not a fancy one. No jumps and twirls, just straightforward and fast skating, racing along the perimeter of the pond until, exhausted, they sat in the shelter to rest.

"You weigh nothing," he said. "It's like skating with a—a—not a feather—that's trite. Maybe a snowflake. No, snowflakes melt." Mike looked at Mary intently. "Like a gauzy handkerchief maybe, kind of floating there over the ice. Next to you, I'm like a Mack truck."

"No, you're not. You're really good. I could only skate like that because you were holding me, and you're strong. Really."

"Yeah? You think so?" He grinned at her. "That's the first compliment you ever paid me. You know that?"

"Is it?" Mary picked at the ice crystals on her glove. "I'm sorry."

"I'm only kidding." He nudged her. "I love to tease you."

Mary blinked. "You must not mind if I tease you," she heard Matthew Hammond saying. "I mean no harm."

"Hey, you look upset. If it bothers you, I won't do it anymore," Mike said.

"It's all right." Mary recovered. "It was just déjà vu. It sounded like something I'd heard before."

"You believe in that stuff?" Mike asked. "Déjà vu?"

"I don't know," Mary said. "I believe there are things we don't understand. Like that report I did on dreams. You know?"

"I remember that. It was pretty far out."

"Yes. Well. I got a letter today from the college where they are doing the experiments." She was flirting with danger, but something drove her on. "They sent some case studies. You want to hear about them?"

"Sure."

"There was a really interesting one about a girl named—Christ—" Mary was tempted to say "Christabel," but thought better of it. "Christine. Christine K. They don't give the whole name. When she started having lucid dreams, she kept finding herself at a certain building. It was a railroad station."

"Like Grand Central?"

"No. This was a small station that existed a long time ago. In her dreams she saw it as it had been a hundred years before."

"Huh?" Mike looked disbelieving.

"That's not all. After she dreamed about the place, she found it in real life. It was practically on her property, but no one knew about it. The building was a ruin, old and run-down."

"You must have got it backward," Mike said. "Surely she saw the old station first, and then she dreamed about it. Power of suggestion."

Mary shook her head. "No."

"How can you be so sure?"

Mary backed off. "I'm just telling you what the case study said. It gets even stranger. Once she had found the station in her dream, she started seeing other things too—like the way her house was a hundred years ago— and the people who lived in it."

"That must have been spooky."

"Oh, no."

"What do you mean, 'oh, no'? If that really happened, it should have freaked her out."

"It didn't. She dreamed about a wonderful couple. She lived with them. Not as herself, as their niece who looked a lot like her—only prettier, much prettier. I guess you could say this girl—Christ—ine—fell in love with these people."

"So what happened?"

"Something . . . made her stop dreaming . . ."

"What, Mary?"

Startled by his tone, Mary jerked back to the present. He was looking at her intently. She threw up her hands and forced a smile. "I don't know. The case study didn't say."

"You really buy this stuff, don't you?" Mike was frowning.

"It's—uh—interesting. That's all." She clapped her mittened hands together. "I'm getting cold."

"Let's skate." Mike got up.

"All right," Mary said.

"You know what?" he said, leading the way to the pond. "Sounds to me like this—Christine—was skating on thin ice." Mike laughed at his joke.

Mary didn't answer. She had already said too much.

Chapter 21

December 30 was clear and cold throughout the day. As party time neared, the sky clouded, and the air became moist.

"I hope it doesn't snow," John Barrone said. "We're having this shindig a night early to keep our guests off the road on New Year's Eve. Be ironic if they ended up driving home on slippery streets."

"Stop worrying." Annie was reassuring. "We can always have a slumber party. I have sleeping bags."

"You wouldn't have enough. You've invited half the town," John said.

"I don't call twenty people half the town. Your father is a worry wart," Annie said to Mary.

The doorbell stopped the discussion. It was Mike.

"What's it like out there? We in for some snow?"
Mary's father shook Mike's hand.

"I hope so," Mike said, smiling at Mary.

"Take Mike's jacket, Brian," Annie said. "And, Mary,
show him where the fruit punch is." Annie gestured
toward the living room.

On a sideboard were two punch bowls and an array
of cheeses and pâtés. "You look nice," Mike said as Mary
ladled punch into glass cups.

Mary looked down, half expecting to see green velvet.
She was wearing a short black miniskirt, black tights,
and a white angora sweater. "Oh . . . thanks," she said.

Out in the hall, other guests were arriving. There was
laughter, Annie's clear voice above the others. Music
came from the sun porch, which had been cleared for
dancing. Balloons floated against the ceiling above. It was
nothing like the holiday ball of 1893.

"This is Mary, our daughter—"

"Mary, have you met—"

"Our boy, Brian—"

"Of course, you know this young lady—"

"Here's your friend, Mr. Gray, Mary—"

Mary's head echoed with introductions from that
other party even as she smiled and greeted her parents'
friends. She moved about, passing hors d'oeuvres, determined to shake off the past.

Mike and Hartley Gray had become friendly during
their visits at the hospital. Annie had seated them with
Mary and Brian at one of the small tables set for dinner

208 ✑

in the living room. They had a fine time swapping stories. Brian kept begging for more. Mary was caught up
in the good humor.

After dinner, Mr. Gray reached under his chair and
brought up a large manila envelope. "Been saving the
best story for now," he said. "It's a corker."

"I hope it's scary!" Brian said.

"You judge." Mr. Gray shook out some papers. "It's
about a feller who lived in this very house a hundred
years ago."

"What?" Mary gripped the edge of the table.

"That playwright." Mr. Gray leaned toward her. "Remember? You asked me to look up Charles Pinkham—
for your school project."

"I'm not doing that project." Her voice rose.

"Gosh darn. That's a shame. Got all kinds of stuff here
from the Dramatists Guild."

"Well, I'm not doing it!"

"Any ghosts?" Brian asked. "Mike tells the *best* ghost
stories."

"It's as good as a ghost story," Hartley Gray answered.
"You may decide to use it after all, Mary." He winked
at her, but Mary didn't respond. Why couldn't he see she
wanted him to stop?

He held up some papers. "This letter thanks us for our
interest in Charles Pinkham. And these"—he handed
them out—"are copies of old theater programs."

Mary looked down at the one in front of her. *Long
Distances*, it said on the cover. The letters began to blur.

This was the play he had been writing. The play he had told her about.

"Pass that one to Brian, Mary."

She looked at Mr. Gray blankly. "What?"

"The program. Pass it to Brian."

She picked it up, but her hand was weak, and she dropped it on the table. Mike reached over and handed it to Brian.

"You like ghost stories, eh, Brian?"

"Yes, sir."

"See that black border? Open the program and read it. You'll find out why it's black."

" 'The Schubert organization mourns the passing on December 31, 1893, of Charles Pinkham, a fine playwright and a great gentleman,' " Brian read aloud.

Mary felt her chest tighten, as if everything she had eaten was lodged there and swelling. Charles had died!

"This is the best part!" Hartley Gray said. "This newspaper article. 'January 1, 1894,' " he read. " 'Word has reached *The New York Times* of the unfortunate and untimely death of J. Charles Pinkham, 38, a premier playwright of this city. Mr. Pinkham was returning by railroad to his home in Riverview, Connecticut, on December 31, 1893. It would appear that he fell asleep and did not hear his station called. Awakening seconds later as the locomotive crossed the Myanous River, Mr. Pinkham, thinking he was still on land, exited the train and drowned. His body was recovered late yesterday.

" 'He is survived by his wife, Julia Pease Pinkham; a

brother, John Pinkham, of Philadelphia; several nephews and a niece.'

"Don't that beat all?" Mr. Gray asked. "What a dramatic end for a man of the theater."

"Wow!" Brian said. "Maybe his ghost will come back to the river tomorrow night. That's New Year's Eve—the anniversary of his death."

"It's a great story," Mike said. He lowered his voice. "And every New Year's Eve at the stroke of midnight a phantom train appears from the darkness, its lights glowing eerily on the ghostly track. Slowly it approaches the river—"

"Where are you going, Mary?" Brian asked.

Mary was on her feet. "I—I—"

"Are you feeling all right, Mary?" Mr. Gray started to get up.

"Yes. I— Excuse me a minute. All right?" She could not think of a reason. "I'll be back." She tried to smile.

"You're not getting overtired, are you, Sam?" At the next table, her father was looking at her, concerned.

"No. No," she said quickly and hurried out to the hall and upstairs.

It could not happen. She could not bear it. Charles was going to die—to drown. And now she understood her dreams and why the train had frightened her so. She had heard the whistle of death.

She went into the bathroom she shared with Brian. She closed the door and leaned against it. Her heart was pounding furiously and there was a ringing in her ears.

She could not go back to the past. She would not go back! There was her family to consider. There was Mike. It was not a choice she could make.

She would just get herself together and go down to the party. She would—what was that saying? She would let the dead past bury its dead.

She shook her head violently, horrified at the thought. If she allowed that, within twenty-four hours Charles would be dead. The article had said he would die on December 31. She looked down at her watch. It was 11:30 P.M. By this time tomorrow night, if Mary did nothing, Charles would drown.

Maybe there was a reason Mr. Gray had told the story. Maybe there was a reason her father had insisted on having this party on the thirtieth instead of the thirty-first. Perhaps it was meant to be that Mary would save Charles.

She pictured Charles, his handsome, laughing face. She remembered him looking down from his tower at her and at Julia in those happier days. The scene was bathed in sunshine, in joy, and she heard his voice calling them. "Julia! Christabel!"

"I'm coming, Charles," she said aloud.

Mary went quietly down the stairs. From the front hall she looked into the living room. Brian saw her and opened his mouth to say something. She put a finger to her lips and shook her head. In the dining room, a couple was helping themselves to seconds of dessert. They paid no attention to her. She went into the kitchen. Annie's white cape was hanging in the mud room. She threw it over her shoulders and ran outside. The wind was blowing, and the gusts intensified as she crossed the yard.

"Charles! Julia! I'm coming back!" The wind drove her toward the stone wall, the cape whipping against her legs. The wind was wrapping itself around her, whirling her in circles about the frozen garden and around the house.

Mary was standing on the front walk. Her voice was lost in the howling of the wind as it whistled around the corner of the house. She was calling their names.

Candles burned in all the windows downstairs, faint oval lights in the darkness. She bent at the waist, pushing against the wind until she was at the bay window, her face pressed against the cold glass.

Julia was standing next to the fireplace under the gas sconce mounted on the wall. She was reading a letter. "Julia!" Mary called as loud as she could. Julia did not look up. Mary rapped on the window. Julia's head snapped back and her hand went to her mouth. She backed up against the wall.

"It's me! It's me!" Mary yelled. "Don't be afraid!"

Julia ran out of the room. Her mouth was moving, but Mary could not hear what she was saying. Mary crouched down, feeling her way along the house until she was at the front steps. She struggled to the door and slammed the knocker with all her strength.

Again and again, she banged it against the door. No

one answered. She called Julia's name, begging Julia to let her in. The wind stung her face, her legs. Her bare hands hurt.

A curtain moved in one oval of the door. Mary threw herself against the glass, her hands cupped around her mouth. "Let me in! Let me in!"

The door opened a crack. "Who's out there?" The voice was harsh.

"Maude. It's me. I have to see Julia." Mary was hoarse, and the words burned her throat.

"Begone now! You'll see no one!"

"Don't close the door. Please!" Mary felt the door pushing toward her. She fought to keep it open.

"You must be mad. Out in this storm, coming onto midnight. Now, go away."

"It's life and death! I must see Julia!"

"Who is it, Maude?" Though Mary's ear was at the crack, she could barely hear Julia's voice. It was thin and frightened.

"Father in heaven, it's an evil spirit," Maude was panting. "Help me close the door. It's trying to get in."

"Julia!" Mary wailed.

"It's a lunatic escaped from the asylum. Go call for help!" Maude hollered.

"I'm not a lunatic. I'm Christabel, Julia. Christabel!" Mary sobbed.

"Christabel! No! It cannot be." There was a sound in the hall, and the door opened. Mary tumbled through it, colliding with Maude, who pushed her back, knocking her into the wall.

Julia was holding a lamp. She held it up to Mary's face. "You're not Christabel!"

"You should not have let her in. I told you she was an evil spirit. Look at her—all in white, like she's come in her shroud from the grave!"

Mary put a hand to her chest and felt the wet wool of Annie's cape.

Maude stepped in front of Julia. "You're not to get near her, you hear?" Hands on hips, she glared at Mary.

"You are not my niece"—Julia's voice trembled—"and I want you to leave."

"It's about Charles. You must listen!"

"Charles? What do you know of my husband?" The lamp in Julia's hand shook.

"He's going to be . . . The train. He will be . . ." Mary could not say the awful words. "He must not take the train tomorrow night! Call him! Tell him!"

"She's babbling. It's crazy she is." Maude moved toward her, hands raised, as if to push her out the door.

"Wait, Maude. Is it possible?" There were tears in Julia's eyes. "Are you his new love come here to cause trouble?" She held up a letter, clenched tightly. "Charles is to return tonight. To reconcile. I don't understand."

"That's not possible. The paper said New Year's Eve . . ."

"Stop your crazy talk." Maude glared at Mary. "The mister will be here right after midnight. That's early enough on New Year's Eve! And not you or anyone else is going to stop this reunion. Now go back where you came from!"

Mary stared at her, stunned. In a few minutes it would be New Year's Eve. That was when Charles was expected, early morning on December 31, not late the next evening, as she'd thought. He was on the train now. "No!" she cried. "No! No!"

Maude pulled open the door and shoved her outside. "Yes. And I'm calling the constable, so you better get off this property!"

It was sleeting and she slipped, fell, and rolled down the front steps. Staggering to her feet, she moved onto the grass. Her leg hurt, but she could move it. She had to run. She had to get to the station before the train.

There was the shortcut from the back yard—she had taken it with Julia. Now, in the blackness, battered by the sleet and wind, she had to find it again.

She passed the dark shape that was the summerhouse and found the opening in the stone wall. On the path, the wind pushed her from behind, and her cape billowed out ahead of her. Icy needles lashed her head and neck.

"Please let me make it! Please!" She prayed aloud to unseen forces. There was no answer except for the wind roaring through the trees. No other sound came from the darkness that surrounded her.

She pounded down the path, and the trees gave way to a field. She must be in the meadow. The storm was worse. There was nothing to break the force of the wind that drove the sleet before it.

Her cape was wet and heavy around her ankles, and she struggled across the field. She came to the wall, but she had lost her bearings, and the stile was not there. She ran

216 ∽

her hands along the stones, expecting any minute to find it. She came nearly full circle before she felt the steps. She sobbed in frustration at the time she had lost.

But then she was on the road. It wasn't much farther. She would get there and save him. The thought encouraged her, and she ran faster.

She became aware that something was different. Another sound was trying to surface under the wind. Like distant thunder, the rumbling began, little more than a trembling in the air. It grew louder and louder, and Mary felt cold terror as she recognized what it was. Now it was joined by the loud, wailing call of the steam whistle. The locomotive of her dream had arrived at the station.

Gasping for breath, she pushed herself to the limit. Ahead was the silhouette of the building. She was almost there when the whistle sounded again. Beyond the building, she could see the train.

"Charles!" Mary wailed, like an echo of the locomotive. She raced around the station where the feeble light of her nightmare glowed through the window.

Whoosh went the pistons. Whoosh. Whoosh. Whoosh. The steam from the engine engulfed the train, and it moved slowly out of the station.

"Stop!" Mary screamed. "Stop!"

No one heard her. The train moved slowly, inexorably, toward the river.

Chapter 22

∽∿∽∿∽∿∽∿∽∿∽∿∽∿∽∿∽∿∽∿∽∿∿

"Mary!"

"Mary!"

The calls were coming from the dark woods. Mary was huddled, shivering and crying, on the broken-down train platform. A loose shutter banged loudly against the building.

"Mary!" The voices were closer now, and she could hear the sound of running feet.

The train was gone, its whistle stilled forever. Charles was gone. The sobs tore out of her throat. She had been too late.

"I see her. She's on the other end of the platform."

"Mary! We're here!"

"Watch out, Mike. Some of the boards are rotten."

Mary lifted her head as the two dark shapes came toward her. She could not stop crying.

"You're soaking wet!" Mike lifted her to her feet. "What are you doing out here?"

"I knew we'd find you!" Brian tugged at her sleeve. "I had this feeling you'd be here."

"Come on." Mike put his arm around her. "We're going to get you home."

"Weren't you scared out here alone?"

"What were you looking for?"

"What'll we tell Ma and your father?"

Mary could not answer. In the past, she had been called mad, an escapee from a lunatic asylum. She had appeared there, blown back out of time.

Now she was here and they were pelting her with questions. *My love is dead,* she wanted to scream. *He will never get home to Julia. Never. Never. Never.*

"They didn't see you leave."

"They didn't see us either."

"They're going to miss us, though."

"Make up an excuse."

"Tell them something."

Tell them he's in the river. Tell them he's in the cold water. Tell them—

". . . that we went out for a walk together."

"In this weather?"

"Gotta think of something."

"She's not making it easy."

Mary could hear their words but had a hard time

fathoming their meanings. She had stopped crying, but her breath was still coming in little shudders. Like a swimmer reaching for the surface after a deep dive, Mary struggled. She could feel Mike's arm. The rain on her face was wet. The air was calm, the trees unmoving. The furor of the storm was over, its energy vanished.

"We're gonna have to tell about the station. Okay, Mary?" Brian's question cut through to Mary's consciousness. "We're gonna say that I wanted to show the station to Mike because of the story Mr. Gray told. See?"

"They'll probably buy it," Mike said. "It's the dumb kind of thing we might do."

"Okay, Mary? Huh?"

Love for Brian swept over Mary, amazing her with its intensity. "Okay," she gasped. "Bri—"

"Yeah?"

"I—thank you."

They straggled home. Brian went in the back door first. "All clear," he whispered. "They're in the front hall. People are leaving."

"You'll be okay?" Mike asked.

"Yes." She did not look at him.

"Sneak upstairs," Brian said, opening the door to the back stairway. "We'll tell 'em you were tired and went to bed."

Mary kissed him on the cheek.

"Don't get mushy," he said.

Mary's legs felt weak. She climbed the stairs slowly, holding on to the banister. In her room, she let her wet clothes fall to the floor, then put on a flannel nightgown and wrapped herself in a terry robe.

The next day she could not even remember getting into bed. Annie scolded her for going out in the rain and risking a cold, but there was little else said about the adventure. It was evident her parents had believed the story Brian and Mike had told them about going to see the station.

Mr. Gray called. He had been out to see the station himself. He told Mary he couldn't get over her discovery. When he asked her to meet him at the Historical Society later in the week, Mary assumed he wanted to discuss the old building.

He had tea made when she arrived. "All right, Mary," he said, once they were settled on a sofa in front of the fire. "What happened the other night?"

The direct question startled her.

"What sent you running through the woods in a storm?" Mr. Gray persisted. "Don't bother repeating the little story Brian told your parents. You left first, and the boys followed. I saw it."

Mary had been miserable all week. It had taken great effort to conceal this from her parents. She had caused so much grief in the past, she was determined not to do the same thing in the present. She needed to talk to someone. She looked at Mr. Gray. He was leaning toward her, a look of concern on his face.

"It had something to do with the story I told, didn't it? And with that wonderful old station you had found?"

Mary nodded. "This is going to sound crazy . . ."

"Trust me, Mary."

"I don't know where to begin."

"At the beginning. That's usually a good place."

"There was this magazine article." Once Mary started, the words poured out. She told him about her early dreams of flying, of seeing Riverview Station. How frightened she had been of the train.

Perhaps she had seen a picture of the station before she dreamed about it, he suggested.

No, Mary assured him. The dream had come first.

She told him about meeting Charles and Julia. About the house and how beautiful it had been.

"You know," he said, "your house is tailor-made for a haunted tale. Out in the country, alone, in need of repair. It would not be unusual that a young girl moving into such a place might be prone to—well, expect strange or weird things to happen. Do you remember what you thought of your house when you first saw it?"

Mary thought back to that late summer afternoon. She remembered the stab of fear as she looked at the summerhouse and the woods beyond. "I didn't like it."

"But in your dreams it was beautiful. Maybe they were a way of coping with your fear and anxiety."

"No." Mary shook her head adamantly. "I saw the house as it really was a hundred years ago. And I saw Charles and Julia. I lived with them." Mary went on to describe the dresses she had worn, the activities she had done—the skating and sledding and partying. "I was there," she insisted.

"Of course it was real to you. I understand. I sit here some days, looking at the pictures, or doing research. Hours go by, and I don't even know it. My body's been here, but I've been somewhere else—back in another time. I know the feeling."

"That's not it!" Mr. Gray's rational explanations frustrated Mary. "There really was a Charles Pinkham," she reminded him. "I didn't know that, and yet I dreamed about him."

He was looking at her over his glasses, chin resting on his hand.

"You don't understand! You don't believe me."

"You have had an extraordinary experience. I believe that. I truly do." He patted her arm. "Don't be upset. Tell me the rest of the story."

She hesitated.

"Forgive an old man's initial skepticism. Go on. I promise you an open mind."

Mary took a deep breath. She sighed. This was the hard part, but she had gone too far not to finish. "I lost control. At first I would decide when to dream. I would do the exercises and make the dreams happen. After a while I would just be there without trying. I would find myself in the past. I was scared, but . . ."

"But?"

"I loved them . . . Charles—and Julia."

"And did they love you?"

"They loved Christabel. Until . . ." Mary looked down, ashamed. "Until Charles . . ."

"I can hardly hear you, child. Speak up a little."

"He fell in love with her. He left Julia and . . ."

"Keep going. You have to finish it."

"He died. Just like you said. He came back on the train, and I couldn't get there in time, and it pulled out of the station, and it was my fault."

"Whoa. Whoa. Whoa, Mary. You're jumping to conclusions. Slow down. How could it be your fault?"

"If I had never gone back, maybe Charles would never have loved Christabel or left Julia or taken the train that night. Don't you see?"

"I see that one way or another you are all tangled up with these people." He pushed back his glasses, which had slipped on his nose. "You have taken on your young shoulders the responsibility of everything that happened. You can't do that."

"What else can I do?"

"Stop blaming yourself. You, Mary, could not and did not alter the past. Even if your dreams were real, they could only happen in the context of what actually occurred. If there was a Christabel—"

"There was!"

"All right, for the sake of argument, we'll say that there was and that Charles fell in love with her. He did not fall in love with twentieth-century Mary—and Mary could not stop him from falling in love with Christabel any more than she could stop a train that ran a hundred years ago. Do you understand?"

She could grasp what he meant. It made sense to her head, but the very heart of her denied it. Mr. Gray had never been there, had never looked into Charles's eyes, had never seen Julia's beauty or felt Maude's hatred. He could not know.

When it was time to leave, Mr. Gray said, "I can see you're still not satisfied. I'll have to try and do something about that."

Mary didn't know what he meant, but a week later he called her on the phone. He asked if he could stop by that afternoon, and Mary agreed. It was Saturday and her parents were at an art gallery. Brian had gone off with Mike, who frequently allowed Mary's stepbrother to keep him company when he was working at the nature preserve.

Mary had not spent any time alone with Mike since the party. She was self-conscious about the episode at the train station. He must have thought it was weird.

Mr. Gray arrived, and she took him out on the sun porch. The sky was a light, clear blue, and though the sun was not strong, the air was soft and pale.

Mr. Gray took papers out of a briefcase. "I've been having a wonderful time," he said. "I feel a bit like Sherlock Holmes." He handed Mary a copy of a newspaper article. "Thought you'd feel better if we could find out what happened to Julia Pinkham."

Mary looked at the paper. It was a copy of a personals column. Two sentences were underlined.

Julia P. Pinkham became the wife of Edward M. Holden in a private ceremony at First Presbyterian Church, Sound

Port, Connecticut, on June 12, 1896. After a honeymoon trip to the West to visit the bride's family, they will make their home in the bride's residence, "Riverview."

"Julia remarried!" Mary said.

"Yes. And evidently she forgave Christabel, since they went West to visit her family. There's more." He smiled and handed her another sheet of paper. "By the way, that explains why I found a record of J. Charles Pinkham buying the house, and a J. P. Holden selling it. Julia was Mrs. Holden by the time she sold the house."

The paper was a photocopy of a birth announcement. It was from the *Sound Port Gazette* and read:

Julia and Edward Holden, formerly of Sound Port, welcomed their new arrival, Jeremiah Joseph, 8 lbs., 3 oz., at 6:00 A.M. on December 31, 1897.

"Julia had a baby." The memory of Julia's sad face when she said she had not given Charles any children instantly came to Mary.

"Four years to the day after she lost her first husband," Mr. Gray said. "See how things have a way of evening out? Julia went on to live her life, and you have to do the same."

"And you do believe me? You would not have looked all this up if you didn't."

"I believe in the possibility. And I'm sure these people existed—for you. But it's time to let them go. It's time to leave them in the past. Can you finally say goodbye to them, Mary?"

"Yes." Mary sighed. "It's over."

He looked at her over his glasses. "Good. For there is someone who cares very much about twentieth-century Mary. And a nice young man he is, too. I like him a great deal."

Mr. Gray was talking about Mike. Coming from anyone else, his words would have embarrassed her.

"I haven't seen him since that night. I'm sure he thinks I'm crazy."

"No he doesn't. We had a little chat yesterday. He stopped by the Historical Society."

"What did he say?"

"Among other things that I'm not at liberty to disclose"—Mr. Gray winked at her—"that you've been avoiding him."

"It's true," Mary admitted. "I was afraid—he couldn't—like me—even as a friend."

"You like him?"

Mary nodded.

"I told him not to give up. Listen, my dear. Take it from an old codger. Every day in the present is precious. You must live life to the fullest."

Mr. Gray's words stayed with Mary. A week later, soft flakes began to fall as she rode home from school on the bus and she repeated to herself, "Live life to the fullest."

She was not surprised when the Jeep pulled up next to her as she walked down Lockwood Lane.

"It's snowing, Mary Barrone," Mike said as he opened the passenger door and signaled for her to get in.

"I believe we have a date," Mary said, settling into the seat beside him.

Mike took her hand and squeezed it.

Mary knew what was going to happen. They would go to the holly grove. The snow would surround them, falling gently on the jeweled trees, covering the ground at their feet. Mike would put his arms around her. Mary would turn to him. He would kiss her while the snow fell softly on their bare heads and their shoulders.

Mary looked out the car window and into the future.